ELEGANT SINS

A DARK SECRET SOCIETY ROMANCE

ALTA HENSLEY

STASIA BLACK

Special Thank you to our editor: Maggie Ryan.

And to our cover designer: Deranged Doctor.

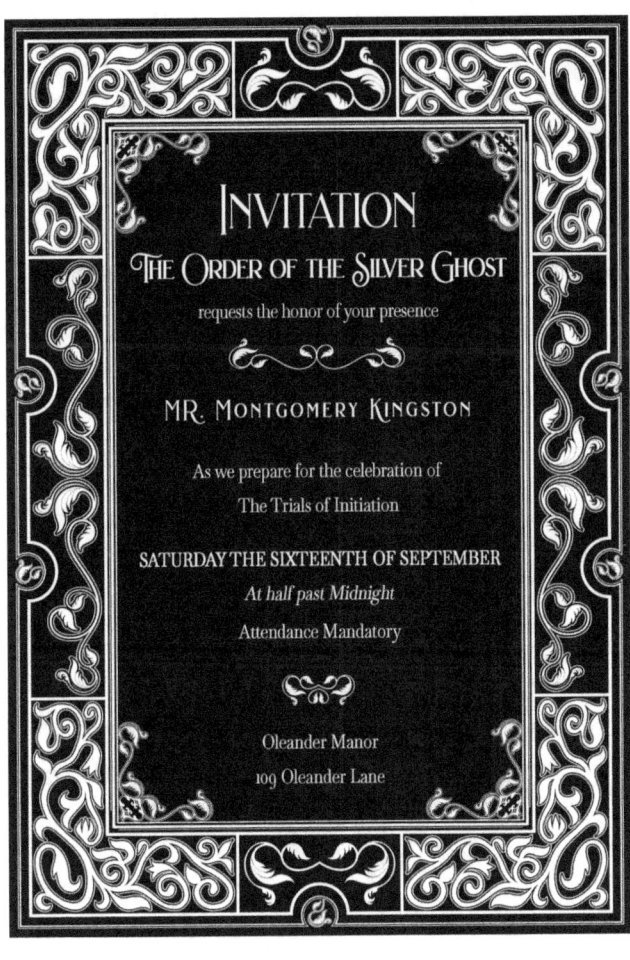

INVITATION

THE ORDER OF THE SILVER GHOST

requests the honor of your presence

MR. MONTGOMERY KINGSTON

As we prepare for the celebration of
The Trials of Initiation

SATURDAY THE SIXTEENTH OF SEPTEMBER

At half past Midnight

Attendance Mandatory

Oleander Manor

109 Oleander Lane

1

MONTGOMERY

B lue-blood lineage had a stench so thick and suffocating that only a true disciple could recognize the smell. It reeked of elegant sins, beautiful lies, and opulent obsessions. The odor dripped with inherited malice, the delicate revenge exacted by the super-privileged on whomever they deemed lesser, and the lavish corruption born of centuries with no one to answer to but themselves.

The fragrance was overpowering.

As I walked down the long halls of Oleander Manor, I breathed in the redolence of expensive bourbon, coveted cigars, and the intoxicating perfume of secret mistresses of times past as well as times present. And although many would be intimidated by such a refined aura, I was at home with it.

Elite.

It was who I was.

What I had been groomed for since my first breath of life.

The Kingston name had eternally represented power and prestige since my great, great, great grandfather. Nothing would change that course other than it would soon be my turn to take over the empire.

I'd waited for this day... for the invitation to arrive.

I knew it would never be as easy as my father simply handing over the keys to the kingdom. I was aware I would have to earn my spot, and although I never knew exactly what that would mean, I understood in due time, The Order of the Silver Ghost would come knocking.

"Gentlemen, I see you all received your invites as well." I said the words deep and loudly. I was taught at a young age that announcing your presence the moment you walked into a room showed a level of confidence needed to compete in the rich alpha society of the South.

Five men, sitting around a circular table, turned to look my way.

Beau Radcliffe was the first to speak casually as he sipped from his tumbler of scotch. "Wouldn't miss it. You're the first of our graduating class to begin the trials. Glad we can watch you fuck it up first so we can learn what not to do."

Ignoring his taunt, I took my seat at the round table made of Honduran mahogany meant for the recruits of the Order.

Six of us.

Up until tonight, we hadn't reached the age or gone through the trials to earn our place with the members. Although since I was indeed the guest of honor for tonight's gathering, it would only be a matter of time until I could leave the *kids' table*.

"Did we have a choice?" Sully VanDoren asked as he seemed to slouch even more in his hand-crafted seat, gulping the booze from his glass as if it were water. The only thing that screamed high-class from the man was the expensive suit he wore accentuated by the tightly closed drapes that hung behind him in a heavy red and gold, so long and opulent they pooled on the floor.

His mama would be so disappointed in his lack of Southern charm. But I expected Sully's sour disposition. Clearly, nothing had changed since we graduated Darlington Preparatory Academy seven years ago. He hated being here, always had, and by the look on his face, always would.

"Why did you even respond to the invite?" Beau asked, not out of judgment but mere curiosity. "It's been years since you've been in Darlington. I figured you were dead or something."

"Or something..." Sully shrugged and reached for the crystal container in the middle of the table filled with a scotch no doubt more expensive than the average Georgian's mortgage payment. "Not my story to tell tonight. This is Montgomery's Trial of Initiation." He lifted his glass to give me a mock toast. "Here's to getting what you've always wanted. Whatever the fuck that is."

"I want the same thing you all do, or we all wouldn't be here," I said.

"Pretty boy Montgomery. Captain of the football team, top of his graduating class, listed in *Forbes* as one of the wealthiest men under the age of thirty, and one of the Kings of Darlington," Sully listed with a smirk. "And now you get to be the first of us to turn twenty-five and be bestowed upon even more. Lucky, lucky you." His sarcasm was not lost on me.

"Stop being such an asshole," Walker St. Claire snapped. "It's not any of our faults you hate this shit, your VanDoren name, and Darlington as a whole. But our heritage and ties to the Order aren't going to go away no matter how badly you might want them to. It is what it is. It's who we are whether you like it or not. And since Montgomery is the first of us to turn twenty-five and begin this process, our time together in this manor is just beginning. So, can we all agree to not be dicks about this?"

I knew Walker would be like me, think like me, and act like me. He too had lived his life as a true Southern gentleman with veins pumping thick with wealth. His father was one of the Elders of the Order, just as my father was, and we both knew that expectations weighed heavy for us to run the Order ourselves one day.

"Anyone have an idea of how much time and commitment this whole Trials of Initiation is going to take?" Emmett Washington asked, looking down at his smart watch. "I have a business to run and am a little short on time to play this gothic game of..."

He glanced around the room, looked up, and smirked. A large Baccarat crystal and brass chandelier hung from the fifteen-foot-high ceiling. Along the ceiling were plaster frieze mouldings that were made from mud, clay, horsehair and Spanish moss.

"I don't even know how to describe this. But I don't have a lot of time to waste on this morbid version of a class reunion."

It was hard not to notice and be impressed with our surroundings. The Oleander Manor was one of the few remaining historical manors in Georgia that had not been burned to the ground in the Civil War. It was so rooted in southern history that you could practically hear the howls of the ghosts without trying.

"Well, it's not truly *your* business until you go through your own Trial," I pointed out to Emmett. His family might be new money, but his daddy had been invited into the Order more than a decade ago. They welcomed all men of influence and power into their ranks—but only men. We couldn't be *too* progressive, now could we?

"We all work for Daddy until the ceremony of the key passing occurs. So, like Walker said, let's make the best of it." I reached for the scotch and poured myself a drink. "Yes, this is going to consume us, but it'll be worth it. We'll soon be richer men than we already are."

"How long do you think they'll keep us in here until we get summoned to the white room?" Rafe Jackson piped in, looking impatient. "I agree with Emmett on having to run a business. I have early meetings tomorrow and don't exactly want to be up all fucking night."

It would be fair to say that Rafe had to work harder than all of us combined. His money was not nearly as old and rooted as we were lucky to inherit, and he had to bust his ass daily to keep the Jackson name on the list as one of the wealthiest in Darlington County.

It wasn't easy to be listed as the richest names in the most affluent county in Georgia, but we all managed to do so. Rafe was one stubborn son of a bitch who wouldn't accept anything but sitting at this prestigious table we all circled around, no matter what it took to get there.

And that was a fact for all of us.

We all would do whatever it took to maintain the wealth for not only ourselves, but for many generations to come.

It was the blue-blood way.

"Never thought I'd see the day that Daddy Kingston would hand over the reins to you," Sully said, eyes dark. "Hit you upside the head with them, maybe. But just place them in your hand with a smile on his face... fuck no."

"He doesn't have a choice," Walker interjected.

I huffed as I took a sip of my drink. "I'm sure it's killing him inside. I never could live up to the man's expectations. No matter how much money I make him, or how much I have added power to his twisted empire, I somehow never do enough."

I glanced at one of the many portraits of the founder hanging above the marble fireplace mantel and felt as if his judgmental eyes were acting as a replacement for my father's. "But rules are rules. The Order of the Silver Ghost have their own law book that supersedes all others. My father can't change the fact that at the age of twenty-five, I get to stop looking in from the outside. If I pass the Trials of Initiation, the business is mine. All of it."

Saying the words out loud felt good. Really fucking good, and I sincerely hoped that my father was somehow spying and listening in on the conversation.

That's right, Daddy Dearest... I will do whatever it takes.

"Talk a tough game all you want, but we all know that what's asked of us is far from normal," Emmett said. Being a relative newcomer, he'd always thought this whole process was nuts. Not that it would stop him from partaking when his time came.

Rafe chuckled as he impatiently checked his watch again. "That's an understatement."

An empty bottle of scotch and a half hour later of small talk, the sounding of a pistol being shot from out in the garden finally announced our night was about to begin.

I took a deep breath but then reminded myself I'd seen all this before.

Yes, we were recruits, but we had attended enough ceremonies in the manor as spectators to know exactly what would come next. Most of us practically cut our first teeth on the ancient furniture in this place. Fathers had brought their sons to the Oleander from the beginning of the Order's creation. We were no strangers to each nook and cranny as well as every hidden and wicked secret the halls possessed.

It was also no surprise to us when a man in a

silver cloak arrived from a secret panel in the wall. "Follow," he said in a low, ominous voice.

Even though we all knew the man was Walker's father, for this evening, he was only an Elder—nameless, faceless, but all powerful. He held one of the highest positions in The Order of the Silver Ghost, and we were expected to treat him with the utmost respect, admiration, and even fear.

In total and complete silence, we obediently followed in single file down a narrow hallway leading us to the white room.

The White Ballroom. The epicenter of it all.

With Corinthian columns, hand-cast archways and an L-shaped extension into a curved bay, the original owner and founder of the order had it painted completely white, including the flooring. It was rumored that the reason was to show off the natural beauty of women who danced within, but also to expose the dark souls and black secrets of all the guests. The founder held nothing back to contrast the good and evil in such magnificent opulence.

Featuring two massive fireplaces with hand-carved rococo white marble mantles, there was also an original mirror imported from France placed so that the women could see if their ankles or hoops were showing beneath their skirts.

Such scandal would never be tolerated.

Oh, how times had changed...

Over one of the fireplaces, there was another painting of the founder, whose eyes most definitely followed you around the room. I hated how the bastard always watched my every move. When I was a child, the portrait would give me nightmares, and to be quite honest, the ghostly picture still did.

Hand-painted German Dresden porcelain doorknobs and matching keyhole covers were the only way to find the exit out since the door seemed to effortlessly blend in with the white expanse. The haunting purity of the room engulfed any who stood within it.

Deep male voices chanted in Latin. What exactly was spoken in hushed murmurs was top secret and only the Elders were privy to that information. Their voices resonated off the walls as we entered the room and stood in line as army recruits would before their General.

Arms behind our backs, legs shoulder-width apart, we stood at attention.

The ten Elders stood before us, their silver cloaks shadowing the features of their faces. Flanked on both sides of them stood the rest of the members, also wearing the silver cloaks belonging to the Order. Each man held an intricately carved cane with a polished onyx ball on top. With practiced perfection, they all began to pound the cane at their feet. The rhythmic beat of the canes rapping the floor reverberated through my bones.

"Montgomery Kingston," one of the Elders boomed. The canes continued to beat. "Are you prepared to begin The Trials of Initiation?"

I nodded, already knowing that recruits were not allowed to speak during any ceremony unless given direct permission.

I stared ahead with emotionless features. I could see in the corner of my eyes that the other five men were taking this as seriously as I was, regardless of how they might have shit-talked about it. It was impossible not to.

If it weren't for the fact that the ceremonies were so rooted inside of us that compliance was just as necessary as breathing, the overpowering dominance in the room would take over any ability to resist.

"You have two days to do the spadework before the Ghost Ball shall commence," the Elder continued as the canes thumped in cadence to the haunting orchestra.

I nodded again.

"You will acquire a belle without equal that night. Then once you do, and we deem her as worthy, The Order of the Silver Ghost will break her."

The canes increased in tempo.

Louder.

Louder.

Wind blew in from the open windows, swirling

around us as if the Order had summoned Satan himself.

The Latin chanting began again as the gas lighting of the room flickered.

"Montgomery Kingston. Your Trials of Initiation shall now begin."

2

GRACE

I looked up when the bell rang above the diner door, signaling a customer. Damn it, I was almost done with my chapter. I scribbled down a couple more notes about Managerial Accounting before pasting on my biggest smile.

Only to look up and see my coworker, Delilah, hurrying toward the counter while juggling her overstuffed purse and tucking her thin white T-shirt into her short shorts—the standard uniform for all the female waitresses at Bill's Diner.

"Sorry! Sorry, I know I swore I wouldn't be late anymore."

She was a skinny girl who liked dying her hair black. She'd been a few years behind me in school, but we'd become fast friends since working here.

I glanced above her head at the clock over the front door. She was over twenty minutes late.

Dark sunglasses covered what I had no doubt were bloodshot eyes. Nobody liked to party harder than Delilah. She was only nineteen, but she looked about ten years older. I glanced behind me toward the kitchen.

I lifted an eyebrow at her. "Just be glad Bill isn't in yet today."

She huffed out a laugh. "As if he'd get off his fat ass and actually work the grill." She leaned over the counter and waved through the little window back to the kitchen. "Hey, Darnell, how ya doing this mornin'?"

She grabbed an apron from behind the counter while she was bent over it.

The diner was fairly empty since it was 10 a.m. on a Tuesday, but Mr. Simmons was a regular. Over his coffee, he took in the eyeful provided by Delilah's short shorts while she bent over. He was a dirty old bastard who pinched my ass every chance he got.

"I'm just fine, 'Lilah." Darnell smiled back.

I just shook my head at her. "Don't let Jimmy catch you flirting with Darnell again."

Delilah pulled back from the counter and glared at me. "Jimmy can go fuck himself. You're so lucky to have Kyle."

Kyle. My boyfriend of three years. There was a time when just his name would've sent butterflies fluttering through my stomach.

Now?

I think of finding him passed out on my couch last night after I'd worked a double, videogame controller still in hand, leftover take-out containers on the table, drool dripping down his chin.

The applications for local positions around town sat untouched on the kitchen table where I'd left them. He hadn't even moved them, meanwhile I was working my ass off to support both of us. And I'd told him not to order takeout. It was the last thing we could afford.

But whenever I tried to bring up money, he just said he liked me better back before I used to bitch and complain all the time. Usually followed by him grabbing a beer from the fridge and walking out of the room.

"Yeah," I murmured, running a cloth over the counter. "So lucky."

"Hey." Delilah's voice was sharp. "I mean it. You got one of the good ones."

I smacked the cloth on the counter and braced my hands, looking up at her. "Did I?"

Then I shook my head at myself. "I always swore I'd be nothing like my mom but look at me, shacking up with the first guy who looked my way." I grabbed the cloth and started scrubbing again, harder than ever.

"You're gonna scrub the Formica off that countertop, you keep going at it like that," Delilah said.

But she crossed her arms over her chest. "And someday you're gonna have to get down off that high horse and realize you're just like the rest of us. Yeah, you're super pretty, but ain't nothing special about you, or me, or any other girl ever born in this county. We were born in the dirt and that's where we'll die. Reading all these books is only making you miserable about that fact."

She thumped my Econ book closed.

"Hey." I grabbed for the book, but she yanked it out of my grasp.

I glared at her. "Bitch."

"Snob."

Then we both cracked up laughing.

She tossed my book back on the counter and reached into her enormous Mary Poppins bag. I swear, her whole arm could disappear into it when she was hunting for one particular item or other, and it was always bursting at the seams. A leopard bra strap hung out of the front pocket. A packet of tissues along with several used ones spilled out as she hunted and finally pulled out a shimmery pink lip gloss.

She was already wearing a siren red lipstick, but she puckered up and smeared lip gloss on top. When she smiled, her cigarette-yellowed teeth clashed with the color, but my grin was still genuine.

"Gorgeous as always. But take off those

sunglasses." I reached over and pulled them off her face. "Bill might be in later and you know he hates—"

I gasped and froze once I saw her face underneath the shades. And the giant bruise blooming around her right eye.

"Delilah! What the hell?" I dropped the glasses on the counter and scooted closer.

She shied back from me and turned her face away. "It's nothing."

"It's not nothing!"

She spun and glared at me, her shiner swollen and puffy. "Jimmy and I just got in an argument last night and it got out of hand."

"Jimmy did this to you?"

I'd kill the bastard. He was twice Delilah's size.

"It's not what you think." She sighed. "I pissed him off. I was snooping around on his phone and he caught me. I really shouldn't have been doing that. He was angry and it went downhill from there. I started shoving him. It really wasn't his fault."

I could not believe the shit I was hearing.

And at the same time, I understood it all too well. Hadn't I heard the same crap from my mom? Over and over. Boyfriend after boyfriend.

He loves me, he just has an anger problem.

It only happens when he's drinking. He's getting help, he swears.

It was my fault. I made him angry. I hit him first; we were hitting each other.

Funny how the guys never came away with bruises or broken bones, though.

"Come on, Grace, don't be like that. You know how the guys around here are. Jimmy got laid off from the shipping center last month—"

"'Cause he kept showing up hungover or still drunk," I interrupted but she ignored me.

"It's not like there's any good jobs around here anyway. It's easier to just drink and forget about it all. Can you really blame them?"

I reached out and took her hand, the dark purples of her bruise looking even more horrendous in the ugly fluorescent lighting of the diner. "Yes. Yes, I *can* blame them."

She just shook her head and pulled her hand back. "You really are such a snob. At least Jimmy's got a steady place to live."

"Only because his mama lets him live in that apartment free."

Delilah just shrugged. "It's better than most guys can offer. I grew up with my five brothers and sisters all crammed into one room of a single wide. So, it seems like I'm stepping up in the world."

And with that, she grabbed the cloth from me and went over to scrub the tables near Mr. Simmons. He lit up, seeing her coming. I couldn't stand him, but Delilah knew how to work him for every spare quarter in tips.

The second she passed by his table, his hand snaked out. I turned away before I could see his gnarled old fingers pinch her butt. After all, I wanted to keep down the little bit of eggs I'd managed to shove in my mouth before running out the door this morning.

Soon things picked up with the lunch crowd and Delilah and I were running our tails off to keep up.

It wasn't until around three in the afternoon before I had another break. I stretched my back. God, it didn't seem like carrying trays of food around should be that tiring, but when the booths filled up, those trays could get really heavy. Not to mention the constant running back and forth.

People would dock your tip for the smallest perceived lack of service. If they finished their coffee and you didn't intuit the very second the last drop slipped down their throat so you could be there with the steaming carafe ready for a refill, they'd get pissed and use it as an excuse not to give you a tip at all sometimes. But if you bothered them too often asking if they wanted a refill, they'd complain you were pesky and intrusive.

Guys liked cleavage on display but if they were with their wives or girlfriends, it pissed the women off to catch their guy sneaking a peek down your tight shirt. Some days you just couldn't win.

I looked at the clock. Just fifteen minutes left on my shift and then I could finally go home. I leaned back against the counter and tipped my head toward the ceiling. Why the hell had I ever invited Kyle to live with me?

At the time, it made financial sense. He had a job back then and we could afford rent on a double-wide if we pooled our paychecks.

Maybe I was just as clueless as Delilah because I thought it was a steppingstone up in the world, too. From single to double-wide. Sure, it was still a house on wheels, but you couldn't beat the square footage. I was going to set up a home office in the extra bedroom to do my homework.

I was almost through with my business degree.

Well, sort of.

It was a degree I'd designed for myself based on the free online business classes from the best colleges in the country. It was incredible how much information there was out there. They just *gave* it away. I'd taken business classes from Harvard, MIT, Stanford, Yale. Courses on entrepreneurship, sales analytics, financial markets.

I did every assignment (even though they were never graded by anyone other than me) and read every book (no matter how long I had to wait for them through interlibrary loan). I wrote papers and did class projects, and I tried to get on every free student forum I could to discuss ideas or swap assignments to grade each other's work.

Not that I'd have a piece of paper at the end of it saying I learned anything or that I was qualified.

But screw that. I knew. *I* knew I'd already finished enough work for an associate degree in business and was now working toward my MBA.

I was smart and I wasn't going to be a lowly waitress barely earning minimum wage all my life.

I looked around the grimy diner. One day I'd own a restaurant of my own and I'd run it right. It would be clean. Bright. A place people wanted to come for a respite from their shitty lives. It would be a place people could spend an hour or two and be inspired that better things were possible.

I'd sell gourmet coffee and provide a wide, exciting menu of dishes so that my customers could experience a flavor beyond Deep Fried. I'd wake up palates and excite imaginations, and I'd build a small enclosed play area outside so it'd be a nice, clean, safe place moms could gather for an hour or two of sanity.

"You've got that dreamy smile on your face again." Delilah elbowed me in the side, and I jerked out of my reverie.

"What?" I felt my cheeks color and I reached for the dishrag to scrub down the counter again, a never-ending task.

But Delilah just grinned. "You dreaming about Kyle? It's about time you two settled down and started thinking about a family."

My mouth dropped open and I could only stare at her in horror. Was she serious? I was only twenty-three years old.

But then her eyes got wistful and she caressed her stomach. "I can't wait until I have a little baby to take care of."

I glanced at her black eye. She'd spent twenty minutes in the bathroom earlier covering it with concealer, but her eye was still shadowed with the bruise. She couldn't actually be thinking of having a baby with *Jimmy*?

"You know Anne-Marie just had her little baby girl and she's *so* sweet. Anne-Marie was so happy when I saw her. The little baby sleeps in bed with them. I got to hold her and change her diaper and she was just like this itty bitty dolly. So cute! And you know, Joe was about to leave her but then she got pregnant and he stayed and now they're both so happy."

Delilah leaned over and propped her elbows on the counter, looking wistfully out the large front window of the diner. "I've always wanted to be that happy."

Dear God, was there any way to talk sense into my friend? Delilah had a good heart. But if she brought a kid into that apartment with Jimmy...

Looking at her, I suddenly had the freakiest feeling that it was like looking at my own mother twenty years ago. Had she been a young woman once just as full of hopes and dreams? Just as hungry for love as Delilah?

Then again, however Mom had started out, the result had been a total shitshow of a childhood for *me*.

A buzzing notification from my phone had me pausing before responding to Delilah. Which was probably good because if I opened my mouth now, whatever I tried to say would come out wrong.

Sometimes I had a hard time keeping my mouth shut. And shouting at her for being stupid and immature and inconsiderate of the life she was so casually talking about bringing into the world rarely won arguments and was why I had so few friends.

I pulled out my phone and glanced down at it.

Then I frowned.

It was a notification from an app I'd installed to monitor my credit score. I'd been meticulous about building up my credit ever since I turned eighteen.

Every business book *ever* talked about the importance of good credit. No one would give me a loan to open a business down the line if I didn't have good credit. I was poor as fuck so I couldn't ever get very high credit lines, but I made sure to open up several credit cards, use them to buy groceries, and pay down the full amount to zero every single month.

So why the *hell* had my credit score dropped hundreds of points and was suddenly flashing red?

I felt like I'd hit a Slip 'n Slide without the water on. All the air was knocked out of my chest.

I stumbled backwards into the counter and gasped for breath.

"Mistake," I mouthed, still gasping. "It has to be a mistake."

I unlocked my phone and scrambled with trembling fingers to get more details.

Ten minutes later, I was outside on the sidewalk, trying my best not to scream at the bank representative on the other end of the phone.

"No, I told you, I didn't make those charges. What the hell would I do with a speedboat? I live in Barnwell. It's hours away from the coast. These are fraudulent charges. And I didn't open those five other credit cards you have on file."

I paced up and down the sidewalk. "How many times do I have to tell you? My identity's been stolen. No, I don't know how or who stole it! If I did, would I be on the phone with you? I tried calling the cops and they said it's outside their jurisdiction! You watch *your* tone of voice! Don't you dare, don't you *dare*—"

The line went dead and I yanked the phone away from my ear, staring at it in disbelief. The bitch had hung up on me. My life was falling apart, and she'd hung up on me!

I let out a scream of fury, ignoring stares from people in the parking lot and on the street. I'd read about identity theft as part of my courses. It wasn't something you could just bounce back from. Once your credit score was fucked, even if it wasn't your fault, it was almost impossible to fix it, and sometimes it took *years*...

"Shit, shit, *shit*!"

I kicked a rock as hard as I could, mostly managing only to stub my toe, before opening my phone back up and going online to look at my bank statement. Whoever had stolen my identity had used my credit card to buy the most ridiculous things.

Other than the boat, they'd basically gone on a shopping spree at a mall outside of Atlanta last weekend, three days ago. $552.98 at Ulta. $3809.52 at Dick's Sporting Goods. $2300.36 at Guitar World. $274.94 at P.F. Chang's.

Huh. That was funny. I'd taken Kyle to P.F. Chang's once when I saved up and we took a vacation to Atlanta. He freaked out, he loved it so much. He swore if he ever got rich, he'd eat at that place every night. It was one of the reasons I wanted to have a more diverse menu in my restaurant.

My head jerked back down, and I looked at the

rest of the purchase history in more detail as an idea popped into my head.

No way. It was ridiculous.

I mean, sure, Kyle did care a lot about his skin care regimen. More than I thought guys ever did. He was always trying to sneak really expensive skincare shit into our grocery cart before I put it back on the shelf. The only way we could afford the rent was if we stuck to a strict budget. Kyle always said I just didn't know how to enjoy life.

And he did always talk about wanting to get a boat someday to "spend a summer at sea" even though he knew nothing about sailing or ropes or driving a boat, nor did we live near a lake or the ocean. Not to mention that he couldn't hold down a job for more than six months, so yeah, we weren't exactly the "summer at sea" kind of folks.

Anyway, I was being ridiculous. Still, I went to my contacts and punched Kyle's name. The phone rang. He didn't pick up.

Why the hell wasn't he picking up?

"Good, you're still here. I need you to work a double."

I looked up to see Bill dragging himself out of his ancient Toyota Camry. There was a lot of Bill for such a small car. First came his meaty thigh, then he grabbed the door and hefted the rest of his considerable bulk out.

He dabbed at the sweat coating his forehead from the effort once he was finally standing and slammed the car door shut behind him.

"Sorry, I can't work tonight." I shoved the phone into the pocket of my short shorts.

Damn it, I should have gotten out of here while I had the chance instead of sticking around to try to figure all this out.

Bill considered you fair game to do whatever he wanted if you were present on his property, labor laws be damned.

I started heading toward my car at a breakneck pace. It was one of my tricks. If I walked fast enough, there was no way he'd be able to catch up with me.

"I said I need you to work a double," he shouted. "And if you don't wanna be out of a job, you'll stay and work."

I stopped in my tracks and swore under my breath. My hands clenched into fists. Still not looking at Bill, I called back, "I'm having a really bad day, Bill. Can I please have the rest of the day off?"

Not even a second passed before his response: "Nope. Paula called in sick again. I need you."

My vision went red, I swear. Paula was a drunk who got into harder shit whenever she could get her hands on it. She was a total crap waitress. But Bill didn't fire her because every time he threatened to, she'd drink half a bottle of tequila and give him a handjob.

Sometimes I hated my fucking life.

I turned around and glared at Bill, hands on my waist. "So, what I'm hearing is that you're screwed unless I help you out tonight." I didn't give him a chance to respond. "So, I'll be back in half an hour. I gotta check on something at home. It can't wait. Delilah's got it till then. See you later.

"You fat fuck," I finished under my breath as I spun on my heel and stomped toward my car.

3

GRACE

This was officially the day from hell.

Fifteen minutes later, I sat cross-legged on my couch, swigging straight from the vodka bottle.

So, Kyle had fucked me.

All around me were the remnants of his hasty exit. His clothes were scattered all over the trailer. The ones that didn't make it into his suitcase, I guess. His Xbox was gone. Along with the TV.

He'd left a note. His handwriting was so shit— it always had been—so it was a little hard to read. He didn't say he was sorry. Like always, it was just an excuse.

You never let me live my dreams. Sandy says I need to choose me sometimes. So, I'm choosing me. Have a nice life. Bye —Kyle

Sandy. I knew the bitch. She'd been the class whore in high school.

Thank God I always made Kyle use condoms. Something he always bitched about, but I wasn't taking any chances. I was on the pill and still made us use condoms. Double protection. I refused to reenact my mother's life.

"Ha," I whispered, looking at the bottle of vodka in my hand. I was doing a bang up job of not being her, day-drinking like this. I slammed the bottle down on the side table and swiped at my mouth.

Shit, how long had I been here? Bill was going to have my ass if I didn't get back.

Blearily, I looked back down at my phone and fumbled until I finally clicked on Uber. Being a little drunk at work wasn't the most professional, but it wasn't like Delilah didn't show up half drunk sometimes. And Paula was a barely functioning alcoholic who had a flask tucked underneath the employee bathroom counter at all times.

There were only a few people who drove Uber in town. I tapped my foot impatiently on the ground while I waited for one of them to pick up.

Finally. And then I saw that it was a Nissan Sentra that was heading my direction, fifteen minutes out. Shit. That meant it would be Jeremy Paulson driving. Jeremy was an asshole on the best of days.

God, I hated living in a town where everybody knew everybody else. Jeremy was a decade older than me but whenever I got him as a driver, he'd spend half the time ogling me in the rearview mirror instead of focusing on the road.

I shouldn't have had the damn vodka.

I grabbed my purse and went to wait outside. Country music blared from the trailer three plots down and Lucia's husband was out with his buddies from the meatpacking plant, all of them set up in lawn chairs around a makeshift fire pit, drinking beers and shouting to be heard over one another.

All the noise *almost* drowned out the sound of Barry and Sheila screaming at each other through the open window next door.

I put my earbuds in and cranked up the music on my phone. Only one earbud worked, though, so it didn't do much to drown out what I'd dubbed Trailer Park Soundtrack.

At least everybody left me alone and finally Jeremy's car pulled in.

I walked up and grabbed the door to the back-seat, but it was locked and it didn't budge.

Jeremy rolled down his window. "Are you Grace Morgan?"

"Come on, Jeremy." I rolled my eyes. "I went to school with your younger sister. You drive me around all the time."

"I represent a global company. It's policy to double check our passenger's identity." He smirked at me and gave me a slow up and down before letting out a low whistle. "Looking fine, Miss... What did you say your name was again?"

Asshole. I was already late and not in the mood to deal with Bill throwing a hissy fit about it once I finally got there.

Apparently, I needed my crap job more than ever now that my credit was shot to shit—because of my own stupid boyfriend. Gah, it was all so fucking infuriating.

Would the police even listen if I presented them with all my evidence that it was Kyle who stole from me? Could we track him all over Georgia, and even if we did find him and that whore he was with, how long would it take to get my credit score back on track?

"If you don't confirm your identity, I'll have to cancel this call and move on to the next one." Jeremy tapped his wrist, not that there was a watch there. "My work is vital to this community, you know."

I glared at Jeremy and bit out through my teeth, "Grace Morgan."

He narrowed his eyes at me. He didn't like my tone. But he unlocked the damn door and I yanked it open before he could change his mind. All these dumb little bastards on their power trips. Bill was the same way. Their lives were so petty, they lorded the stupidest shit they could over others and thought it made them men.

All it really did was expose how weak they were.

Give me a man *worth* respecting and I'd fall at his knees.

Ha. Too bad they didn't exist.

"Take me to Bill's," I said, not taking my earbuds out. Hopefully Jeremy would take that as a cue not to try small talk.

His unhappy eyes met mine in the rearview. "Don't you mean *please* take you to Bill's?"

Every cuss word was on the tip of my tongue, but I'd had enough practice at work on how to choke them back.

Still, I couldn't help making my smile overly saccharine as I grinned at him in the mirror, clasped a hand to my chest, and asked, "Please, dearest Jeremy, will you pretty please take me to Bill's Diner in this most worthy conveyance?"

He frowned, sensing I was making fun of him but not smart enough to be sure.

Either way, he finally put the car in drive, and we started down the county highway toward Bill's. Thank God.

Leaning against the seat, I tipped my head back, closing my eyes. I turned the volume up on the music, pretending to be asleep or that the music was too loud when Jeremy tried to make conversation several minutes later.

I only opened my eyes when the car came to a stop. I sat up and looked around, pulling the earbuds out of my ears.

"Where are we?" I asked, frowning when I saw we were in town, but still about half a mile from Bill's.

"You should be nicer to me."

I sat up straighter. Was he fucking serious?

"I'm late, Jeremy. Take me to work. Now."

He hit the steering wheel and I jumped at the noise. "That's the kind of shit I'm talking about. You need to be grateful. You wouldn't have been able to get to work if I hadn't come and picked you up."

"It's your job. You work for a company and that's the service the company provides."

He scoffed. "Yeah, well it's only me, Terry, and Ramirez who actually drive, so chances are, you're going to get stuck with me a lot. And I'm thinking it's time you started showing some gratitude."

My vision went red for the second time that day. "And I'm thinking it's time you go fuck yourself."

I slammed the door open and got out of the car, yanking my purse behind me. But I wasn't done. "I'm not going to take this harassment anymore, you small-dicked little bastard. Neither are the other women of this town." I was yelling now and attracting stares again, but I didn't care.

Jeremy's face turned red with fury, but he was noticing the people watching, too. His window was still rolled down from earlier.

"Everyone in town thinks you're a stuck-up bitch so just get off your high horse." His face contorted in an ugly smirk. "You're hot but no one wants such a whiny cunt around. Gossip is Kyle split town with Sandy. Now I see why."

Then he drove off, spitting dust and gravel into the air. I flinched as some of it hit me, throwing up my hands to protect my face.

For a second, I could only stare after he left.

And all I could think was that my car was still at home. What if Jeremy picked up when I clicked on Uber to go back home?

That was it. I was officially *never* drinking vodka again.

I started trudging down the sidewalk toward work. There was nothing else to do except keep going forward, right? One foot in front of the other?

It took me another twelve minutes to walk the half-mile to get to Bill's, and I was sweating by the time I walked in. I pulled my long, dirty blonde hair off my neck and tied it into a ponytail as I pushed the door open with my backside.

A loud cacophony of voices immediately

greeted me. Shit. That meant the dinner rush was already hitting.

"Where the hell have you been?" Bill's voice rang out from the kitchen. "Get your ass in an apron and take over Section 4."

Oh goody. So, the day from hell looked like it was just getting better and better.

I passed by Delilah and she lifted her eyebrows at me, giving me the warning look we passed each other when Bill was in an especially bad mood.

I nodded and scurried to put my apron on. Grabbing a pad and pen, I raced over to Section 4.

"How can I help you today?" I asked, smiling my sunniest smile at four large men in their 40s or 50s who'd crammed themselves into a booth closest to the TV we turned on in the evenings that blared ESPN.

"We have been waiting here ten minutes already and no one asked us what we wanted to drink," complained the guy in the corner, his trucker hat slightly askew.

A red-faced guy nearest me, bald on top except for a few wisps combed across his shiny, greasy head, spoke up next. "But now we got this hottie who's gonna work her ass off to make up for that if she wants any tip at all, ain't that right, baby?"

He wasn't even subtle about reaching around to pinch my ass. And the motherfucker pinched *hard*.

I couldn't help the little yelp of surprise that escaped but he only grinned wider.

I smiled just as broadly back, already planning to ask Darnell to add some "special sauce" to whatever this fucker ordered.

"Happy to brighten your day," I said through my teeth. "Now, what can I get for you? Why don't I tell you about our specials today?"

And that's how I managed to get through the next few hours. Running my ass off, bullshitting my way through bad customer behavior, and avoiding Bill at all costs.

That was, until he cornered me after the dinner rush slowed down and I paused for a bathroom break.

I stepped out of the bathroom and Bill was standing right there, blocking my path.

"What kind of stunt do you think that was earlier, running off when I needed you?"

God, I was so tired. I couldn't remember the last time I felt so bone-weary. "Look, Bill. I'm exhausted. Can we talk about this tomorrow when I come in?"

That was the wrong thing to say. I knew it immediately by the way his face darkened.

"Who do you think you are? I'm the owner of this place and you're nothing. You're less than nothing. I could replace you like this." He snapped his fingers.

I bit my tongue. Bill wasn't Jeremy. I couldn't just go off on him.

As much as it sucked, I needed this shitty job. There was so little opportunity for work in this town, it had taken me four months to get hired here.

The only other place in town was the shipping facility, but I'd heard nightmares about working in that place. Same with the meatpacking plant and that was an almost forty-five minute commute. Not to mention that when I *did* earn good tips and worked doubles fairly often, I could manage rent and just a little extra.

I looked down at the floor, pretending a subservience I sure as hell didn't feel. "I'm sorry I was late, Bill." The words were acid on my tongue, but I said them anyway. "You might've heard, but Kyle left me today. I just had to go home and see if it was true."

By the noise of surprise that came from Bill, I guess it was news to him.

"He left you?"

I nodded fervently. Bill wasn't an especially sympathetic guy, but maybe he'd go easy on me just this once. I had legitimate cause for emotional distress, even if missing Kyle wasn't the reason I was distressed.

"And he stole from me. So, I'm sorry I was distracted today. I just had a lot on my mind."

"Well." Bill blinked. "Don't let it happen again."

I nodded. Thank God. Maybe Bill would let me off the hook. But he still wasn't moving out of my way, so I waited to hear what else he had to say.

"You know, I've been waiting for this day," he finally said.

What? What did he mean by that?

But when I looked back up again, Bill was already settling a hand above me on the wall. A wave of body odor assaulted me with the action, but Bill seemed oblivious.

"That boy was never right for you. You're a real pretty girl, ya know? I always envisioned you with an older man. Someone who could take care of you right. Someone who owns property. Who owns a respectable business."

Bill leaned in, and now I could smell his foul breath in addition to his armpit odor. His teeth were yellow as he smiled at me.

Oh God, he couldn't be suggesting—

"I always thought you and I had a sort of special relationship. Now that Kyle's out of the way, I think we should—"

The bell rang over the door of the diner. "Oh my gosh, I told Delilah that I wouldn't leave her alone out there."

Without another word, I forcefully squeezed my way underneath Bill's arm and all but ran out to the front of the diner. But Bill moved with me and rubbed his body all against mine as I passed, and I didn't miss the stiff bulge in his pants that he pressed against my pelvis as I went.

Ugh. Full body shudder. I'd need to take a bath in Clorox when I got home.

My mind was so fixated on what had just happened outside the employee bathroom that it took me a second to register the man who'd just walked in the diner.

But when I saw him, I paused. So did everyone else in the room.

Because what on earth was a stranger, dressed in a tuxedo—such a formal tuxedo that it even had *tails* to the coat, no less—doing in a podunk diner in the middle of Nowhere, Georgia?

By the look on the older man's face, he was just as discomfited to be here as his outfit suggested.

"You lost?" someone called out to him.

"I accept!"

My head swung around, and I was shocked to see that it was Delilah who had shouted at the fancy stranger. She was whipping her apron off over her black hair and all but sprinting across the room to the tuxedo'd man.

"I'm here! I accept! Delilah Monroe, at your service."

In the whole time I'd known her, I'd never seen Delilah look so excited. Her face was lit up, her features childlike with joy. She jumped up and down. "I accept! I accept!"

Was this guy from the lottery? Or some kind of sweepstakes and Delilah had just won?

She stuck her hand into the man's face. "Where's my invitation? I accept!" She laughed with giddiness.

But the man's expression didn't budge. He looked at Delilah like someone might an animal at a zoo. Like she was a creature of little interest and he was already bored with her.

While she was still jumping up and down, the cool-eyed man began to survey the rest of the room. He looked to be in his late fifties, early sixties at the latest. His skin was tan in a way that belied his fine duds—like he'd spent plenty of time outside. But the way he held himself and the elegant way his gray hair was pomaded back spoke of a cultured background at odds with the patch of red on the back of his neck from recent sun exposure.

This was definitely the most fascinating thing that had happened at Bill's in recent memory and frankly, after the day I'd had, I was happy for the distraction the stranger provided. I leaned against the counter and watched to see what would happen next.

But I was completely unprepared for the stranger's eyes to stop on me and pause in recognition. I glanced behind me, sure he was looking at someone else. But there was no one there.

And when I looked back, he was already walking in my direction.

"Miss Grace Magnolia Morgan. I am honored to convey this invitation."

He bowed in front of me—actually *bowed*—and then handed me a thick, cream-colored envelope.

"What is..."

But I took the envelope because what else do you do when someone hands you something?

"We look forward to your attendance."

With that, he turned on his heel and left the same way he'd come.

What the hell was that? Murmurs immediately broke out across the diner. People picked up their phones and started texting. I had no doubt the gossip about the mysterious stranger would be all over town within the hour.

Suddenly the envelope in my hand felt like it weighed a hundred pounds.

I ripped it open and then felt terrible about tearing the beautiful paper envelope. There was even a red wax seal on the back.

But I couldn't stop. I yanked out the single sheet of paper inside. It was heavy card stock and reminded me of a wedding invitation. Was that what this was? Was I related to someone rich and I just didn't know it? Like, they'd hunted down even obscure family to invite to a fancy wedding they were having.

But when my eyes skimmed the wording of the invitation, I was only more confused.

THE ORDER OF THE SILVER GHOST
Requests the honor of your presence

MS. GRACE MAGNOLIA MORGAN

As we prepare for the celebration of *The Trials of Initiation*

MONDAY THE EIGHTEENTH OF SEPTEMBER
At half past seven in the evening

OLEANDER MANOR
109 Oleander Lane

Attendance mandatory

What the hell did that mean?

"What's it say?" someone called.

"Let me see!" said another.

"Pass it around!"

I pressed the card to my chest and looked around. Every eye in the diner was on me. I looked for Delilah. Black tears ran down her face as her mascara ran in dark rivulets down her cheeks. She looked crushed.

I strode over to her, grabbed her hand, pulled her outside and around the edge of the building toward the alley. She was the only one who seemed to know what was going on.

"Delilah, what does this all mean?"

"It means"—she hiccupped and swiped at her eyes, only smearing her mascara more—"that you're the luckiest girl in the world."

"We've got to get back." I looked over to the diner. "Bill will—"

"Fuck Bill," Delilah waved my concern off. "Do you even realize what just happened back there? Oh my God, your life just changed, and you don't even realize it yet. You can be so dumb sometimes."

"Hey!" I smacked her arm.

"Sorry," she said, crossing her arms. "But I would kill for the opportunity you just got."

I lifted the invitation. "What is it?" I looked back down at the invitation. "Seems like some sort of prank."

Delilah's hand smacked across my mouth. "Don't disrespect The Order of the Silver Ghost. They're probably listening to us right now."

I looked around at the abandoned alley and lifted a disbelieving eyebrow at my friend. Maybe she'd been getting into more than just hard liquor lately.

"Don't look at me like that. I'm serious. They're powerful."

"Who are they?"

"No one knows. It's a secret society. And they take their secrecy real serious."

"So how do you know about them?"

"Oh, everybody knows about them." She waved a black-fingernailed hand at me.

I scoffed. "Some secret society."

"Shut up." She leaned in. "What I mean is that everybody *whispers* about them. The men want to be members and the women, well, the women... What you're holding in your hand right there"— she sighed, leaning against the side of the brick building and looking longingly at the invitation in my hand—"is the golden ticket to a new life."

"But what does that *mean*?"

Delilah pushed off the wall and got right in my face. "It means that you follow the directions on the invitation exactly. You go where they say. You wear what they say to wear. You do what they say. You do not talk back. For once in your life, Grace, you'll have to shut the hell up and just *obey*."

Whoa, whoa, whoa. Stop the bus. "*Obey?*"

I took a step back from Delilah, but she followed me, a determined look on her face. "They'll give you whatever you want. You dream it up, they can give it to you. I've seen it happen. The women walk away, and all their dreams come true."

"What are you even talking about? None of what you're saying makes sense."

"Oh my God, don't be so precious." Delilah looked disgusted with me. "So, what if you suck some cock for a few months and take it up the ass a couple times? Are you listening to me? You can get out of this town! After three months, you'll be free to do whatever you want, all the money in the world. You get to name your price. They can make anything happen for you. *Anything*. The sky's the limit with these guys."

I just stood there as my mouth dropped open. "You want me to be a... a *prostitute?*"

Delilah rolled her eyes. "Oh my God, it's not even like that. Some of the women who come out say it's the best sex of their lives. Plus, the men are *rich*. The bluest of the blue bloods. They're *ultra* rich. They run politics around here, the police, you name it. Just *think* of what you could do with that kind of money and influence. One woman started a multinational corporation that does relief for starving children in Africa. Isn't that the kind of do-gooder shit you want to do?"

Damn it, that had me stopping in my tracks. That was far bigger in scope than I'd ever imagined. My dreams had always been small. Local. But what if I had money? *Real* money?

I had no power in this world. Hadn't today taught me that?

I wanted to help others, but I couldn't even help myself. I thought about earlier outside the bathroom. Bill apparently thought breaking up with Kyle meant he had full rein to move in. He assumed he had the right because of his measly amount of power over me.

Say he kept cornering me until I either finally gave in and started giving him hand jobs like Paula did, or I quit, and looked for somewhere else to work.

Just some other dead-end job where I'd no doubt get groped, too.

All the men in this town sucked, but I liked sex, and what if one of them eventually managed to knock me up? Condoms broke and the pill wasn't a hundred percent. What fresh hell would I be in for then? Stuck to some loser with a kid I could never give the life they deserved, working a job I hate and forced to put up with handsy bastards all my life because I. Had. No. Power.

Or...

"It's just three months?" I bit my lip.

Delilah's face lit up. She nodded fervently. "Oh my God, tell me you're going to do it. One of us has to get out of this shithole."

I threw my arms around Delilah and pulled her close. She smelled like cigarettes, stale beer, and coffee.

"I swear if I get money and get out of here, I'll come back and get you. If this really is a golden ticket to my dreams"—I felt ridiculous even as I said it—"I'll come back and bring you with me to my new life."

But when I pulled back, Delilah was just smiling at me sadly. "No, you won't. You'll forget all about me. You'll wipe this town off your boots and never look back. And I won't blame you."

I stared at her hard, vowing she was wrong.

I wasn't sure what I was getting into. I doubted there would be a pot of gold at the end of the rainbow like she thought. In my experience, anything that sounded too good to be true usually was.

But life had me by the balls. I knew exactly what I was getting if I stayed on the path I was on now.

Or I could risk everything. Leap into the unknown.

And God knew I was clever, but I'd never been especially smart.

Because I was going to accept the invitation.

4

MONTGOMERY

Getting my affairs in order wasn't as difficult as one would think. Maybe it was because I had been preparing for this day my entire life, or maybe it was because as much as I wanted to believe I played a crucial part in the running of my family's business, I really wasn't all that vital.

At least not yet.

I also knew that I could still run all my daily tasks for the most part from within the walls of the Oleander. In fact, in many ways, closing deals and conducting others would be easier. Now that I was truly becoming a sanctioned member of The Order of the Silver Ghost, my level of... dominance... was about to intensify.

I wasn't just being handed the keys to the kingdom. I was about to have tools of mass destruction bestowed upon me. Montgomery Kingston would soon be a name not a soul would cross. And I wouldn't have to do a thing to earn that notoriety other than exist.

But there was one thing I needed to do before I would be locked up in my temporary cage. Saying goodbye to my mother was a must.

Was I a mama's boy?

Call it what you would. I had no shame in my actions, my devotion, or my respect for a woman who would throw herself on a sword for me.

"Well, look who finally showed his face," my mother said as I approached her on the back porch. "I had a vacant seat next to me in church today. You should have seen Pastor Green looking at me with condemnation all over his face for not having my son present."

I leaned down and kissed her cheek. "I know, Mama. I'm sorry. I had a lot to do today to prepare for…"

I wasn't exactly sure how much my mother knew of The Trials of Initiation. It would be tricky testing the waters on this. I knew everything about what I was about to do was supposed to remain confidential, but I also knew my mother wasn't completely naive to the Order. "I just had a lot of work to do that couldn't be pushed off."

"Well, since you aren't going to be attending church anytime soon, you should have made a point of it to come today."

She motioned for me to sit down in the rocker beside her, a small white table between us. It was our usual spot after Sunday service.

"But regardless. I prayed for the both of us." She glanced over at me with a smile in her eyes even though she desperately tried not to smile with her pursed lips. She could fake she was mad at me all she wanted. I deserved it. Sunday was the one time of the week that I tried to give to her, and I didn't expect her to simply let me off the hook no matter what the reason.

"I bet you were praying for a long time," I said as I looked over her shoulder at a small-framed brunette woman wearing the usual Kingston uniform the entire staff were required to wear, but I didn't recognize her. She was young and pretty, but they all were. My father wouldn't have it any other way.

The housekeeper brought a pitcher of lemonade and two glasses, placing them on the table between us. She refused to make eye contact, and I could see how her hands shook with unsteady nerves.

"Thank you, Leeza," my mother said.

"It's Liza, ma'am." Her correction came out so softly that if it weren't for the fact that my mother still had impeccable hearing, she would have missed it.

"Oh yes, yes, sorry. Thank you, *Liza*."

"Is there anything else I can get you, Mrs. Kingston?" Her hands fisted in front of her as she subserviently looked to the ground. I'm sure my father loved when she did that around him.

"That will be all for now." My mother flicked her wrist to dismiss her, and although it was a sign of a woman who hadn't had to wait on herself in decades, it was also a show that my mother was not attached to the woman and for good reason.

"She's new," I said as I poured the lemonade.

"Third one this month. I'm getting to the point where I don't even care to remember their names, but then I'm going to look like some old lady losing her memory if I don't. You know your father. He's so particular and demands a lot."

It took all I could do to not roll my eyes and huff. Yes, I knew my father. And yes, he had many demands. All of which involved taking advantage of his poor house staff. I was pretty sure it wouldn't be long until I saw the housekeeper's face in the halls of Oleander Manor. I had seen so many of our house staff eventually become mistresses of my father or his colleagues.

It was a secret I kept from my mother, but not really. She knew. I knew she knew. We all knew. The Kingston way was to act like we all didn't.

If you don't speak it, then it doesn't exist.

"Why have you always allowed him to do the hiring and firing?" I asked.

Shrugging, she said, "He runs a tight ship. Only room for one captain. It's easier to pick your battles, and who we have working for us is not a battle I care to engage in."

It often bothered me how much my mother allowed my father to take control, but at the same time, I admired her grace and ability to not fight and create tensions in the household. There was a wisdom in the way she handled my father. An acceptance that I tried to master, but often failed at.

She wasn't a weak woman... nor particularly submissive. She was simply comfortable in a role she chose. It was as if they had a silent contract that bound them in life, society, and family.

Just not devotion. And whether or not they loved each other or ever had... well that wasn't a question one asked in polite society.

My father was a son of a bitch who cheated on her constantly. But he never did it in public—only at the Oleander Manor—and never to embarrass her. And he didn't treat my mother poorly. She was his most prized possession. His diamond. He put her on a pedestal and then enclosed her in glass, like a piece at a museum.

If Mama had ever questioned her lot in life, I'd never seen it. I'd had a happy childhood. She was always full of smiles. It was only as I'd gotten older that I realized she knew everything else going on while Dad was out of the house—which was a lot —recognized it for what it was and decided to leave it alone. That took strength, not weakness.

But he was still a son of a bitch.

"109 days is a long time," she said as she stared straight out at our expansive estate. A large weeping willow tree dwarfed all else, and it was hard not to stare at anything but.

I nodded, grateful that she clearly knew enough that I didn't have to walk on eggshells not to reveal Order secrets while saying my goodbyes.

"Did Father tell you it's my turn? I got the invitation."

"He didn't need to. I know you're of age, and I've been around this world long enough to know exactly what happens in the halls of the Oleander."

She glanced at me, and my expression of shock must have been written all over my face. I'd suspected she had a vague idea of the goings on there, but the conviction she spoke with suggested more intimate knowledge.

She laughed softly. "Don't be so surprised. Even though the wives aren't part of the Order, we aren't completely blind. Not to mention, I happen to be good friends with Mrs. Hawthorne. You don't think I would have allowed you to go to the manor as a child if the housekeeper wasn't a woman I trusted to look out for you and the other boys, now would you? Her Irish temper kept you boys in line, and I know she'll still watch over you the same way."

Remembering Mrs. H chasing us down the halls with threats of thrashings if we broke anything as we played tag made me smile.

"I have no doubt she'll still keep a good eye on you while you stay there."

I was far from a boy needing looking after, but knowing there would at least be a familiar face while residing in the manor did help ease my anxieties... because yes, 109 days was a long time to be away from everything I knew and loved.

"Has Father said anything to you about it?" I wanted to know how he felt about being so close to handing over the business. He was a workaholic, power-hungry, and not one to give anything unless it benefitted him. I couldn't imagine him being too pleased about this tradition.

She took a sip of her lemonade, the ice clinking against the crystal the only sound for several minutes. "You don't need to worry about what your father thinks now. You're a grown man."

In other words, he was pissed off. My mother never lied to me, but she wouldn't be so honest to say exactly what I already knew.

"I've been working for him my entire adult life. I'm ready."

"Yes, you are."

"And you're right, I don't have to worry about

his feelings, but it would be nice for him to communicate, or give fatherly advice, or even a sliver of praise at least once in my goddamn life." My blood began to boil, and even sipping on the chilled lemonade couldn't cool it down.

"You're the man you are because of your father. You wouldn't be nearly as strong, capable, or determined if it weren't for the fact that you wanted to prove something to him. Your need and want is what gave you all the power."

She turned her head and looked at me directly in the eyes. "I'm proud of you. I know I'm not your father, but I am so very proud, and I hope that means something to you."

"Mama, of course—"

"Hush, let me finish." She grasped my hands. "I'm not just proud of all the accomplishments you have achieved on the surface. You are a good, good man. Your soul. Your heart. Your mind. I raised a man who can't be topped. You are a true Southern gentleman in every sense of the meaning."

"I don't believe you would think so if you truly knew what I will be expected to do in these trials." I wasn't even completely sure what would be required myself—future recruits were only allowed in on some of the Invitation events—but I knew enough through rumors and dark tales to know it wouldn't be something a mama would be proud of.

"I know more than you think, and I want to

stop you right now if you even for a second start feeling guilt. Those women who attend the ball, and the woman you choose to go through the trials with you are not forced. They know exactly why they are there. The Order of the Silver Ghost are the kingmakers and the dreammakers You will walk out of that manor a king."

Her fingers clutched around mine. "That woman will walk out of there with her dreams come true. She is there because she *chose* to be. *Chose to*. I want you to remember that."

The kingmakers and the dreammakers. How true that was.

"What if I'm asked to do something I am morally against?"

Her jaw tightened as her eyes darkened. "You will be."

"You said it yourself, that I'm a good man," I reminded. "Am I supposed to just forget that part of me because of the Order?"

She shook her head. "There is a very fine line between good and evil. Everyone has a seat in their soul for the Devil. The trials will pull the chair out and invite the dark angel to sit."

She leaned forward. "And though the man you go in the manor as tomorrow will be pushed to a breaking point, and you will indeed tango with the demons inside of you, you'll come out mightier and more in tune with the real person you are.

You'll see the completed portrait. All the shades and shadows blended with the light from before."

"And the poor woman who agrees to this? What about her?" It felt freeing and slightly scary to even ask the questions out loud, hesitations I hadn't even admitted to myself. It had always been like this with my mother. She was the one person on earth I could say anything to. "Maybe she'll have no idea what her acceptance to the invitation really means."

"True. She has no idea. Not really. But that's the point. She'll also have to dance with the demon. And the goal will be to break her. Shatter the woman she believed herself to be. She won't be the belle of the ball without having to earn it. And the price is high."

I sighed, hating the Order, despising tradition, and loathing my lineage for the first time. Why couldn't I just be handed the family business like a normal man who had earned the title?

Why couldn't my father just pat me on the back and tell me how honored he was to have his son right by his side?

Instead, I had to go through this ritual of sin.

"I want you to remember something, Montgomery. Every little girl grows up loving the fairytale of Cinderella or Beauty and the Beast. They all want their Prince Charming and their happily ever after. Some women will never get that perfect narrative. For many, it will simply be nothing more than a childish bedtime story. When the invitations are sent out to all the surrounding counties, though, this is so many young ladies' chance at being plucked from nothing and given everything they ever dreamed of. It's win-win."

I nodded silently, agreeing with that statement.

"And yes, what the Order does to them... what *you* will do to someone... may have them walk down a very dangerously corrupt lane. But keep reminding yourself that there will be a happily ever after for that woman in the end."

"Would you have done it before marrying Father? Accepted an invitation?"

She chuckled, her eyes drifting back to the willow tree as if gazing back into the past. "I was a rich Southern belle by birth. My path was already chosen for me. Unlike those women who get the invites, I didn't get to choose my fate. Wealth, arrangements, and the Southern way did that for me."

She rocked back and forth in her chair, the wood of the floorboards beneath her creaking loudly. "And though you have grown up with privilege as being the only child of the Kingstons, and you have had so many opportunities in life, I often wonder what it would have been like for you if wealth, arrangements, and the Southern way didn't control your life as well."

I stared at my mother, again shocked by her words. I thought she was content with the sacrifices she'd made in her life, that she was more than satisfied by her place in society and on all the charity committees she filled her days with. Then again, lately she had been spending more time working with her hands in the dirt amongst our extensive gardens rather than out doing the society circuits.

"Mrs. Kingston," the housekeeper said softly as she walked onto the porch, interrupting our conversation. "Mr. Kingston just called to inform you he wouldn't be home for supper tonight. He said he would be home late and not to wait up."

Mama kept rocking in her chair, her cool elegance as stately as ever as she inclined her head ever so slightly without looking at the girl. "Thank you, Liza."

"Is there anything you would like for supper in particular, Mrs. Kingston?"

"It doesn't matter. Whatever is in the refrigerator."

"Will your son be joining you?"

I cleared my throat. "No, thank you, Liza. I'll have to be leaving shortly."

Liza left and I turned my attention back to my mother. "You gave me a wonderful life, Mama. I love you for it."

She reached over and patted my hand. "I know

you still have a lot to do, so I don't want you to feel you have to visit your old mama any longer. But promise me something."

"Yes?"

"When you feel you have lost your soul in the rooms of the Oleander—and trust me, you will—I want you to know you haven't. This entire process is a fairytale. A dark, twisted, and depraved tale you will be experiencing. But there will be a happily ever after. Keep telling yourself that to maintain your sanity."

"I promise."

"And one more promise," she added. "Allow yourself to truly explore the deep, hidden desires inside of you. Don't hold back. Discover the bad. Explore the side of you that has always been suffocated by Southern charm. This is your time to be broken too. Don't fight it."

"All right, I will."

I said the words because I knew it was what she wanted to hear. But to be honest, I had no idea if I truly believed them myself. I had no idea what I would be walking into.

I only knew one thing. I had 109 days.

109 days to endure a rooted history interwoven with thorns and strangled with poison ivy.

5

I woke up the next morning and everything was... the same.

Because duh, obviously.

Last night, Delilah had made it all sound so dire and important. But now that I blinked my eyes and looked around the dingy master bedroom of my trailer, the dirty brown carpet, the peeling linoleum of the bathroom that I could see from my bed...

I flopped back on my pillow.

I was such an idiot. Some weirdo in a Halloween costume probably high on meth came into the diner last night and gave me a pretty piece of paper—and of course Delilah romanticized the hell out of it and got dreams of grandeur.

It was probably just a prank. The Order of the

Silver Ghost. The name sounded familiar, so I googled it when I got home last night. There are conspiracy theories about it, but they all sound as fake as crap about the Illuminati.

I wanted out of my life so desperately, I was willing to grasp at straws.

But I wasn't Cinderella and there was no such thing as dreams come true.

A sudden banging at the front door had me jumping out of my skin.

"Jesus!" I covered my beating heart with my hand as I climbed out of bed and yanked the robe from the hook on the back of my door.

"Coming!" I called even as I squinted at the midmorning light. God, what time was it? It was the first day in forever that I didn't have a shift and I'd been looking forward to sleeping in. The microwave clock said it was 9:23. Who the hell was banging on my door at 9:23 in the morning?

I swung the door open without even looking. And froze in my tracks.

It was the guy in the Halloween costume from last night. Starched white tuxedo shirt and black coat tails, his graying hair perfectly coifed. He was holding a huge white box that almost engulfed him.

"What the hell are you doing here?" I crossed my arms over my chest.

He lifted the huge white box toward me. "Do you accept the dress? The ball is tonight. You must arrive three hours early, prepared and wearing everything in the box."

I just stared at him for a long moment.

Until finally, he pressed again. "Do you accept, Miss Morgan?"

"Are you for real?"

A small smirk quirked the older man's lips. "I assure you, Miss Morgan, I am very much real. As is the invitation you received yesterday. Do you accept?"

I swallowed hard, then laughed and brushed my hair back from my face, leaning out and looking around. Where were the cameras? Where was the man jumping out saying this was all a joke or some sort of weird reality show?

There was no one there, though. Just Jeeves here, and for once, a quiet trailer park. At this time of morning, everyone was still sleeping it off from the night before. But soon they'd start waking up, and what would I say if anybody saw this guy?

"I thought the invitation said attendance was mandatory." Was I stalling for time while I tried to figure out what to do? Yes, yes, I was.

The Jeeves lookalike just looked at me cryptically. "There's always a choice." Then he was back to his same old line: "Do you accept?"

There was a rustling down the way. Damn it. Mrs. Brown always was an early riser. She loved nothing more than spreading gossip around the park community. This fancy guy in his fancy tux standing outside my door at 9 a.m.? By noon the whole town would know if I didn't get rid of him fast.

So, I made a split decision. It was all probably still a hoax anyway.

"I accept." I yanked the huge box away from Jeeves, pulled it in the house, and slammed the door closed in his face.

Ten minutes later, my jaw was still on the floor.

It was the most exquisite dress I'd ever seen.

I thought I'd seen fancy dresses before—at the mall, and once when I went to Atlanta and walked beside some upscale shops. I mean, some of those dresses were over $100. I'd even dared touch one dress that was $180.

But this dress...

I reached out with the tip of my index finger to caress the delicate little gemstones hand-stitched onto the bodice but then pulled back at the last second. What if the oils on my finger damaged it? It seemed like a work of art that I might screw up at any moment.

I immediately ran to the kitchen sink and washed my hands and then washed them again.

Then I came back to the box.

Holding my breath, I lifted the dress out of the box. My breath caught. I'd never held anything so luxurious or beautiful in my entire life.

It was a dress for a princess. Like some Disney shit but in real life.

My hands shook as I held the gown up to myself. I couldn't be sure, but it looked like it was a perfect fit. Not a sample size, but the size of an actual human woman with hips and a bust.

How did they know my size?

I glanced back down in the box and my eyes opened wider. It wasn't just the dress. There were also underthings inside.

I looked around for somewhere to put the dress down, but nowhere in my dingy trailer seemed clean enough.

Finally, I took it to my bedroom, pulled back the comforter, and laid it down on the sheets. I'd just put new ones on, wanting to exorcise Kyle from the place. It was the cleanest spot in the house.

With one lingering glance at the dress, I scurried back to the box and bent over it again.

I swallowed hard and slowly reached down inside. The dress had been a dainty, pale blue.

But the underthings? They were siren red.

First, I picked up the bra. It was a fairly standard push-up balcony bra. It would make my tits look great. But then there was also a freaking *corset*. An actual corset.

I frowned and picked up a few stringy bits left at the bottom. What on earth...

I dropped it immediately again when I realized it was the itsy bitsiest thong I'd ever seen in my life. And were those... stockings and a garter belt?

I breathed out long and low.

Holy shit. If this was all... real... then I was in way over my head.

Wasn't I?

Because the dress might be Cinderella, but all this stuff was much more in line with Anne Rice's dirty version of Sleeping Beauty. Yes, I read the books. Yes, they were hot as hell.

But I'd only had sex with a few boys. High school boyfriends and then Kyle. And while occasionally Kyle liked it doggie style, most of my experience was pretty vanilla. One high school boyfriend was addicted to porn and had a difficult time staying hard for me—an actual live girl—so we did it a few times, but he preferred blow jobs. Kyle usually just climbed on top and hammered away until he finished, got tired, or passed out. I got off sometimes, though more in the beginning than any time in the last year.

I backed away from the box.

This was all moving really fast.

Delilah had mentioned *anal*. My hand moved to my butt and I flinched.

This was all ridiculous anyway. I tried to laugh it off. It wasn't real. Then I wandered back to my bedroom and stared down at the dress that had to be worth more than two months of my salary. Maybe three.

"Holy shit," I whispered, biting my bottom lip. Then I grabbed for my phone and dialed Delilah.

"Of course it's real." Delilah rolled her eyes at me an hour later, pushing past me into my trailer. "*Duh*. Oh my God, let me see the dress."

I swiped the cup of coffee out of her hand. "No coffee near the dress. It's in the back bedroom. Wash your hands if you're going to touch it!"

But she was already off like a shot. The next second, all I heard was a girly scream. "Oh my *God*! It's an Aristides de la Fiallo dress! Do you know how much these things cost? Have you tried it on?"

I hurried back to her side. "No, I haven't tried it on. Of course I haven't tried it on."

Delilah looked at me like I was crazy. "Why not? How much time do you have before the ball?"

"The ball starts at 7:30 and I have to be there three hours before, so I have to be ready at 4:30."

Delilah gasped. "Why didn't you say so? We barely have any time!"

I arched an eyebrow. "What are you talking about? It's not even noon. I was thinking maybe we could go out to Mama's Waffle House and talk through my options. I'm still not sure if this is something I want to—"

But Delilah just started laughing. "Don't be silly. You already took the dress. You already decided."

"What are you talking about? Jeeves said it was my choice."

"Who's Jeeves?"

I waved a hand. "It's just what I call the tuxedo guy with the invitation."

"Anyway," she continued like I hadn't said anything, "it was your choice. But then you accepted the box. So, I'm sure they started the process."

"What process? How do you know so much about this?" I felt lost in the wilderness, but Delilah just treated it like it was all normal. I was starting to think they'd picked the wrong girl. She would've been perfect for this. She was sexually adventurous and, like me, had nothing to lose.

"Well, you're starting a new life. And you can't exactly live two of them at the same time. So, if you get chosen, they'll shut this one down." Delilah waved all around us. "And if you want to know the truth, I know it all because it happened to a friend of my favorite aunt. She got the invite when she was about your age."

"Wait. What? How long ago was that?"

"I don't know. Twenty years ago, maybe."

"This has been going on for twenty years?"

Delilah laughed at my credulous expression. "Don't you get it? It's been going on for way longer than that. Hundreds of years. It's a way of life for these rich guys."

Hundreds of— "They just go around buying women? That's disgusting."

"My aunt's friend didn't think so. Especially when she got to live the rest of her life in a mansion on the French Riviera, where I might add, she later fell in love with a *duke* vacationing in France. Now they live happily ever after."

"That sounds made up."

Delilah's eyebrows shot to her hairline. "It's true! Look. My aunt is still friends with her on Facebook. I'll show you."

Delilah pulled up her phone and scrolled, then shoved it in my face.

I frowned but took the phone. On it was a woman who looked like an aging model—her beauty was still clearly visible, just wearing a little around the edges.

She grinned widely at the camera as she leaned into a distinguished-looking gentleman with an arm around her shoulders.

They looked so... *happy*.

And rich. They looked rich as sin. There was a mountaintop chalet in the background. It was probably easy to be so happy when you were also so rich.

"I'm telling you, Grace, you'll be around men who are really powerful and influential. You can have whatever you want."

"Said the spider to the fly," I murmured.

"What?"

"Nothing." I waved her away and breathed out heavily. "All right. So, where do we get started?" I looked down at the gown and then thought about the box full of underthings.

I'd never know if I could do this until I tried.

"First, we have to start with your hair and makeup. Go take a shower and blow dry your hair. I'll get out my makeup box I brought with me. I've always wanted to do a makeover on you!" Delilah clapped giddily and did a little spontaneous dance.

I took one quick peek at her heavily made up racoon eyes and winced. I could only hope for the best, right? I barely wore any makeup and had certainly never done glam makeup before.

I'd just have to trust that Delilah could restrain

herself. I smiled at her. "I put myself in your capable hands."

Delilah nodded but was already pulling out all sorts of creams and eyeshadows out of her makeup caboodle. "Don't you worry about nothing. I'll make sure you're the belle of the ball."

I looked like the bride of Frankenstein.

Sad but true.

I didn't have the heart to tell Delilah she'd gone overboard on the eye makeup, especially when she was so extremely proud of herself when she'd stepped back earlier and said, "Ta da!" urging me to go check myself out in the bathroom mirror.

I didn't look anything like myself, it was true.

And if tonight went as disastrously as I thought it might, maybe that was a good thing. Nobody would know who I was, and I could just sneak away with my tail between my legs.

It really was a shame about the dress, though. Because the dress was a true work of art. And the way it fit my body...

Delilah had made me put on the dress before I looked at myself in the mirror so I could get the full impression. Thank God for that, because I'd been about to cry once I saw the clown-like makeup.

Then there was the dress. It hugged the curves at the top of my body before billowing out in a cloud of organza. It looked like I was dancing even though I was standing still. The slightest movement made the gown shimmer.

Then there was a knock on the door and Delilah was squealing about a limo outside.

I'd never seen a limo in real life, much less ridden in one.

But here I was, two hours later, trying not to gawk but finding it impossible. My hand lifted to the glass of the backseat window almost without my volition.

The drive up had been impressive enough. At first the landscape had been familiar, normal. Other than the fact that I was in a limousine. Who on earth had a limousine in Barnwell, Georgia?

But soon enough we weren't in Barnwell anymore, were we? No sir, we were in Darlington now.

Everyone in Georgia knew at least a little about Darlington. It was part of the slim strip down the middle of Georgia that hadn't been burned in the Civil War.

Rich people from Atlanta had their second homes here, massive estates that belied so much of the poverty of the rest of the South. It was Georgia's secret little Mara Lago, nestled right in the center of the state. No beaches but plenty of golfing and sweet tea as far as the eye could see.

I should have guessed this was where I'd be coming.

I shifted uncomfortably in my poofy dress, anxiously trying to smooth out any wrinkles. The invitation said to wear it, but maybe I should have just worn normal clothes and brought it in the box it came in?

Because as I passed through the wrought iron gates, opened by two footmen in full livery like something out of Downton Abbey, it hit me full force.

This was real.

It was all very, very real.

Rich men wanted to buy me—ostensibly had *already* bought me—and would do whatever they wanted to me behind these gates.

I was a nobody with no voice and they could just—

Make your dreams come true. Any dream. Delilah's words ricocheted through my brain.

"Fuck," I whispered under my breath as the limousine continued forward down a smooth, freshly-paved road that was lined on either side by ancient oak trees, planted at regular intervals every twenty feet. Their branches stretched like arms embracing in a canopy over the road, blocking out the bright sunlight.

It was an impressive and forbidding sight. Those trees had been planted purposefully, hundreds of years ago. On and on they went, the Avenue of Oaks, calling me closer to my destination. My heartbeat sped up as we turned a final corner and the house—no, the *mansion*—came into view.

I don't think I breathed for several seconds.

I'd never seen anything like it. Even in movies. Even in fairytales.

Even in my dreams.

I didn't know to dream that big.

I looked up. And up. And up.

Huge, stately square white columns lifted up into the sky like a modern day Coliseum. Except everything was perfectly intact. It was like stepping into history. It was only two stories tall, but each floor was massive, with a huge wraparound deck. Everything was done in elegant whites and grays, with black wrought iron railings on the balconies and patios. Black shutters completed the dramatic look.

And did I mention *massive*? Because holy shit, as we drove closer, I just kept seeing more and more to the building. Or maybe there were multiple buildings? I couldn't tell if it was just one giant structure that wrapped around or if it was a network of interconnected buildings. Either way, it had to be tens of thousands of square feet large.

Who the hell lived here? Surely no one person could own such a place. But it wasn't a historical landmark, either. At least not one I'd ever heard of. People were crazy for their Southern history in these parts, and this place had never come up on any of the class field trips or anything else I'd ever heard about even though it was only a couple hours away from where I grew up.

I didn't know much about architecture, but this place had to be, what? At least 100 years old. But for as big as it was, it was probably pre-Civil War. So that meant over 150 years old.

My gawking was cut short though, when my door suddenly opened.

There was Jeeves, looking as calm and unperturbed as ever. He held out an arm to me. "Miss Morgan."

Oh shit. I'd been distracting myself with details of the house but here Jeeves was, throwing my actual situation in my face again.

"What if I don't get out of the car?" I squeaked. "What if I ask you to turn around and take me back home? Will you do it?"

He sighed impatiently, the first time I'd seen him do anything like break character. "Back home to what, exactly?"

My mouth dropped open for a moment. "I have

a life. I might not be rich"—I gestured lamely to the huge mansion in front of us—"but it's a life and it's my own."

"Miss Morgan, the correct procedure is to wait until you are inside, but since you're already here, I'll ask you now. What do you want?"

"What do you mean? Look, I'm just asking if you'll take me home."

"Is that what you want?" he peered at me curiously. "What do you really want out of life? To go back to your life—a life that is 'all your own,' to use your words. No one is forcing you to be here, Miss Morgan. If you stay, you do so of your own free will. But were you truly free?"

He leaned in ever so slightly. He had to be dying of heat in the September sun, dressed to the nines like he was, but he didn't bat an eye.

"I had a glimpse of your life, Miss, and pardon if it is not my place, but it didn't exactly look like freedom to me."

He pulled back. "Inside you will be interviewed. They will ask you again what it is you truly want. You can ask for anything. You are Aladdin and we are your magic lamp."

"But it comes at a price," I said emphatically.

Jeeves just looked at me like I was being foolish. "Do you think you deserve to be given something for nothing? That's the way a child thinks, Miss Morgan."

I nodded, biting back curse words on the tip of my tongue. I wanted to lash out at the guy, tell them all to go to hell, and run away before I got in too deep.

Maybe it was cowardly. Maybe it was prudent. Maybe it was my gut telling me to get the hell out of here.

But Jeeves was right about one thing—living paycheck to paycheck didn't feel like freedom. And I couldn't keep going back and forth like this.

I swallowed hard and looked back up at Jeeves, the afternoon sun so bright, I had to squint. "The men. Are they very horrible?"

I couldn't be sure, but I thought maybe his face tightened just the littlest bit?

"There are rules to protect you. You will have a safe word that you may use at any time." He stood up straighter. "But know that if you do use a safe word, it's all finished. You will be immediately removed from the house. You forfeit your prize. You get nothing. There is no partial credit. But the choice is always yours. You may leave at any time."

I blinked rapidly at that. "Do... do girls leave often?"

"I've worked here eleven years, and it's only happened once."

"Out of how many girls? How often does this happen? What happened to the girl who went home?"

He smiled and I couldn't read him. "That's enough for now. Will you enter?" He held out his arm once again.

I felt like Alice peeking down the rabbit hole.

Half of me wished I'd never seen this man's face. That he'd never walked into the diner with that damned piece of paper and offered me this weighty choice.

But then I took his arm and he led me up the drive toward the intimidating mansion. A little further. I'd go a little further. I could always say a "safe word" and stop at any time, right? I could go back to my boring little life where nothing exciting ever happened. Where I had few choices and even fewer options of actually getting ahead in this unforgiving world.

"Let me introduce you to Mrs. Hawthorne," Jeeves said.

I didn't trust myself to speak, so I nodded.

Instead of leading me up the half a dozen stairs to the grand columned porch, however, Jeeves suddenly detoured to the left. I tottered along unevenly after him, unaccustomed to the three-and-a-half inch heels that had also come in the box. Several times, Jeeves had to reach out a hand to steady me. He was gracious enough not to comment about it.

He guided me around a cobblestone pathway that led past the east wing of the house, right up to a small white door that had a little placard over top that read: *Servant's Entrance.*

Were you even allowed to still have signs like that up these days? It was *so* not politically correct to call someone a *servant.*

But when Jeeves knocked once, the door was immediately opened by a plump white woman in her 50s, her graying red hair pulled back in a severe bun. She was wearing a starched gray dress with a white collar and a white apron, and she didn't look happy to see me. In fact, she outright glared as she eyed me up and down.

"As soon as you step over this threshold," she finally spoke, her words as severe as her hairstyle, "every moment will be a test. Just like you were tested from the moment you received the invitation."

Her words took me aback and I looked to Jeeves, but his face was impassive, giving me no information one way or the other.

"The invitation told you to prepare yourself appropriately." She gave me another long once over. "An instruction you failed." She glared down at the tiny watch on her wrist. "There will barely be time to fix it in addition to the interview and the inspection."

She glared over my shoulder at Jeeves. "You could have at least driven faster once you saw this disaster." She gestured up and down at me.

"Hey," I said, stepping up in Jeeves' defense. "It wasn't his fault. And I"—I cringed a little thinking of my raccoon eyes—"maybe if you could just help me take off some of the eye makeup?"

"You"—Mrs. Hawthorne's eyes snapped back my direction—"silence from now on." Her thick Irish accent made her statement come across even more authoritative.

I looked to Jeeves. He'd been my guide through everything so far. But he was checking his phone, obviously done with me now that he'd delivered me, and his responsibility was through. He'd told me himself, hadn't he? He'd worked here eleven years. How many women had he seen come and go?

"W-What's my safeword?"

One of Mrs. Hawthorne's thin eyebrows went up. "That will be up to you and the gentleman, obviously. My job is to prepare you, to make sure you are clean and safe."

Okay my makeup might be a little bad, but did she think I didn't shower? What the hell? I was poor but I was still *clean.*

"This way." Mrs. Hawthorne tugged me forward by my wrist and closed the door in Jeeves' face.

I only got a glimpse of the kitchen and a bunch of staff inside all bustling around, dressed in crisp kitchen whites.

Meanwhile, I was hustled up a steep, narrow

staircase that had to have been for servants and earlier, for slaves.

Nor did I get to see much of the second floor before I was hustled into a small room. Immediately, Mrs. Hawthorne flipped me so that I was facing the door she'd just shut behind us, her hands at the zipper of my elegant gown. I tried to look over my shoulder. There was a narrow bed but not much else in the room.

"What's going on?"

"I already explained myself and I don't waste my breath saying things twice," Mrs. Hawthorne snapped.

She pulled the dress down my shoulders until it billowed at my waist. "Step out." She held out a sturdy arm to steady me. I used the wall instead.

She swept the ball gown away the moment I was free of it and hung it on a hanger in the room's tiny closet.

"Knickers off," she commanded, never once looking my way, not since we'd left downstairs.

"Um... what?"

Finally, she looked at me, and it was a look of exasperation. "Don't tell me you're modest. Not if you're going to be one of the Order's girls." Then she rolled her eyes. "Every few seasons we get one of you."

She propped her hands on her waist and stared me down. "You are here for sex. The boys will be undergoing the most important trials of their lives and you will not"—she took a step forward, one menacing finger pointed in my face—"I repeat, you will *not* screw up that opportunity for them. You will do as you're told. You will suck cocks, you will be fucked more times than you can count, and you will do it all with a smile on your face."

I blinked in shock at her blunt words. She'd seemed so... grandmotherly when I first met her at the door. Like a mean grandma, the kind who yells at neighborhood kids when they're having fun, but still. Hearing the words *cock* and *fuck* come out of her mouth—

"Stay like that," Mrs. Hawthorne went on. "A lot of the men in the Order like that innocent Bambi look you've got going on. And one of my favorite boys comes of age tonight. If Montgomery Kingston chooses you, you better treat him right. He's got a lot to prove, and he needs a whore who'll spread her legs, suck his cock, and do everything she can to help him thrive in every challenge."

"I'm not a whore!" I breathed out in shock.

Mrs. Hawthorne scoffed out an unkind laugh. "There's a reason they don't marry your kind. But the Order's fair. You'll get your paycheck in the end."

I blinked and bit my bottom lip against her unkind words.

She leaned in near, her hawkish nose even

sharper up close. "You gonna cry, little girl? I thought they did their research and only picked the resilient ones."

I locked my jaw and tilted my head at her. She was a mean hag who liked to pick on people when they were down. I'd known people like her my entire life, including my own mother.

Instead of spitting curses, though, I smiled sweetly. "Well, I guess I better make sure to ask for a big enough paycheck then, huh? If I'm going to suck all that cock, I better make it worth my while. Are you the person I tell how much I want, or do I discuss that with my" —what was the word she used earlier? Oh right— "my gentleman?"

She was back to glaring. "It's part of the intake process." She looked down at her watch again. "Which you are distracting us from. Go ahead and strip completely naked. You'll have to bathe from scratch because you've also made a disaster of your hair. There's nothing to be done for it. So, strip and wait on the bed for the doctor. I'll come for you afterwards to bathe you."

Bathe me? I wasn't five. And— "The doctor?" I squeaked in confusion, but she was already whirling away in a flurry of gray skirts and sensible shoes out the door.

A doctor was coming to "inspect" me. Jesus Christ. They knew I wasn't a virgin, right? What else could a doctor— Ooooh, was *that* what she'd meant by clean?

I felt like an idiot. I was here for sex. Of course they'd want to make sure I wasn't diseased. But wasn't it a little too late for that? Shouldn't that have been one of the first things they asked instead of the last?

I looked down at myself in the expensive lingerie. Shit. Mrs. Hawthorne had kept going on about how I was late and wasting time. But was I really just gonna strip down for some strange person who said he was a doctor to put his hands all over me?

Then again, Mrs. Hawthorne said everything was a test. And I wasn't doing too well at following instructions, was I?

Without thinking too much more about it, I started stripping down. Still, I did pull the afghan from the bottom of the bed and wrapped it loosely around myself for cover once I was completely naked.

The doctor didn't knock before coming in, but I was relieved when I saw it was a woman.

"Hi, I'm Dr. Nichols." She was young, maybe just in her early 30s, and shockingly beautiful. She tugged the stethoscope from around her neck and reached out to shake my hand. Her skin was a deep ebony, she had short cropped hair that only accentuated the long, gazelle-like beauty of her neck.

She smiled easily, a huge bright smile that had me easing off my guard in spite of myself.

"Hi, I'm Grace," I said tentatively.

"Hi, Grace. There's a lot coming at you really quickly, huh? I get that all of this is crazy and intense. I'm just here to check out your vaginal health and run some quick blood tests. The Order has your bloodwork from when you saw your doctor six months ago, but they just want to double check that you're still clean and disease free. The men undergo the same check. They really are committed to everyone coming out of this experience with no permanent reminders." Her smile was compassionate.

I had only about a jillion and one questions.

"So first let's take your blood and we'll shoot it off to the lab." She opened a case she'd brought with her and started pulling out supplies.

"How do you know all this?" I blurted. "Doesn't it take a long time for lab work to get results back? And wait, how did the Order have access to my personal doctor's records? That's confidential information."

Dr. Nichols smiled at me as she had me sit before she tied the rubber tubing around my arm. I still clutched the blanket around myself. "I can't say much, but I am allowed to tell you that I went through the process myself. And as you can see, I came out on the other side just fine."

"What?" I jerked a little as she jabbed the needle in my arm, and she shushed me. "Shh, stay still or I'll have to keep sticking you to find the vein."

I nodded and settled. She found the vein with the second try. My blood began to fill up the vial.

"I'll talk but only if you stay still."

I was about to nod but stopped myself just in time. "I'll stay still," I whispered, barely moving my lips.

"Excellent. Look, I understand that you're scared and confused. I really do, believe me. But just let yourself go along with the process. Don't try to anticipate. Just give in to it. There's no shame or judgment here. As cliché as it sounds, try to take it one day at a time."

"What was it like?" I whispered. Now that I had a real, live person in front of me who'd actually been through this, whatever *this* was, I wanted to know everything.

She just smiled at me, a coy, gorgeous smile. "To be honest, it's different for everyone. It depends on the gentleman who selects you. But trust me, you *want* to be selected. It'll change your life."

Her eyes clouded, went distant. "I didn't have a very good childhood..." It was the first time since she'd entered the room she wasn't smiling.

But then she shook her head, like she was coming out of a trance. "Then I got my invitation, and everything changed." The smile came back. "Now I'm a respected OB/GYN in the city. I'm engaged. Happier than I ever thought I'd have a right to be. So, I come back here to help out and to encourage you girls."

She finished with the last vial of blood and pressed a cotton ball against my arm before putting on a small Band-Aid. As she worked, she continued to talk, "Mrs. Hawthorne might seem like a tyrant and it's true, some of the men in the Order are dogs and won't treat you much better. But there are rules and the ones being initiated aren't like the older men who've been in the Order forever."

She finally met my eyes. "Basically, Grace, you just have to be careful. You have to trust your gut. You have to be smart. Can you do that? If you don't think you can do that, you should leave now."

I looked up at her, so glad to have someone finally give it to me straight. Between her and Mrs. Hawthorne, I felt like I had a much clearer picture of what I was getting myself into.

If I were going into this, it would be with eyes wide open.

Slowly, I nodded.

"All right." She smiled kindly. "If you're ready to continue, then lay on the bed and I'll be right back."

She placed the vials of blood into a small,

chilled container and then left to hand it to someone who was apparently waiting right outside the door. She returned and then urged me to the edge of the bed so she could start her examination.

"We don't have a lot of time, so they've asked me to combine your interview with the inspection. I've got a voice recorder here you can hold." She gave me the handheld device before replacing her gloves.

"Open wider." Her voice was professional as she nudged my thighs open and reached for the speculum.

"Now, state your full name clearly into the audio device, along with what it is you want at the end of this experience." She lifted her head so I could see her above my blanket-laden thighs. "And don't forget to dream big." She gave me a wink.

I thought for few seconds, and then pushed the button on the side. "My... uh... name is Grace Magnolia Morgan, and I—"

The cold speculum made me jump when it made contact with my skin, even more when she clicked it several notches open. I couldn't help hissing out in surprise. It had been a while since I'd had sex. Could she tell? Was it obvious? If she could, would that be points for me or points against? Did it matter at all?

"Just tell them what you want, Grace," Dr. Nichols said from between my legs.

Right. Not awkward at all. *Just talk about your life goals with a speculum up your hoo ha, Grace—no biggie.*

So, as best I could, I tried to enumerate every hope I'd ever had for myself, finally putting a dollar figure on my dreams.

Everybody I talked to said to dream big, so I did.

To get a business degree from a respected university and to open a restaurant in Atlanta with enough capital to make it through the first critical two years without fear of running out of money, plus enough to live on—

"Ten million dollars," I finally finished on a gulp right as Dr. Nichols pulled out the speculum. "You can have me for ten million dollars, and I'll obey whatever order I'm given. But that's my price. Ten million."

Perfection. Flawless.

Two words I used to describe how I functioned in life.

Two words that were both my strengths and my weaknesses. The need to achieve both at all times could cripple a weaker man, but I was far from weak. I knew that growing up with a silver spoon in my mouth would lead many to believe I had everything handed to me, when in fact, it was quite the opposite. My father made me earn everything.

Every single thing.

Even his love, and I had yet to do that.

I was not a spoiled rich boy who never had to work a day in his life. Even at the age of twenty-five I felt as if I had worked a lifetime.

Battle worn.

Seasoned.

Perfection. Flawless. My motto in life had gotten me far up until this point.

Although, as I stood in my tailor-made, all white tuxedo with a matching bow tie, I felt far from perfect and flawless. The pure white of my surroundings nearly suffocated me, and yet I felt soiled and marred with the tar of wrong doings of past, present and future.

The ballroom was white, the recruits who would soon have a ball of their own were also in white tuxedos. The only color in the room were the silver cloaks the Elders and members wore.

White and silver.

Ghostly in an elegant way.

"Are you ready to choose the unfortunate belle?" Sully asked as he walked up to where I stood and patted my back. "Blonde, brunette, or do you like the redheads?"

I didn't respond. It sickened me the way Sully made it sound as if I were about to choose cattle for one of the ranches my family owned. I couldn't let him get in my head. We were all gathered and ready, and it was just a matter of minutes before they would begin the ceremony.

"Want a drink?" Sully asked as he held up his whiskey straight. "I sure as hell would need it if I were in your shoes."

I shook my head and glanced at the white, intricately carved grandfather clock that mastered the room. The hands of the face were golden sabers, adorned with tiny rubies. I'd loved that detail as a young boy, but tonight they seemed... deadly. "I'm good."

"Leave the man alone," Walker said as he walked up and stood next to Sully and me. "This shit is intense." He looked at me closely, examining my face. "Are you doing all right? Anything you need?"

"A fucking drink is what the man needs," Sully said as he finished off his own in one big swallow.

I disagreed. It was necessary for me to remain sober and on top of my game tonight. I had no idea what to *truly* expect. I had a pretty good idea of the basics since much of the ceremony and Initiation tasks were spelled out in the Order's law book. But I wasn't so naive as to believe I was prepared for what would come, not only tonight, but for the next 109 days.

I don't think anyone could be prepared for The Order of the Silver Ghost. The inherited malice of the ceremony felt like a noose around my neck, but regardless... it was about to occur whether I was ready or not.

The clock struck midnight, and if it weren't for the loud hammer strike of twelve chimes echoing through the room to notify us of that fact, the Elders and their canes were sure to. With each peal of the hour, the canes beat in cadence against the white floor.

"Bring in the belles," one of the Elders demanded after the twelfth punch of his cane.

The recruits lined up with me in the center of the room. We stood at attention and waited. I wondered if the others were holding their breaths as I was or if that would come on their night. Maybe they were grateful it was me and not them.

I actually wished I wasn't the first of my group so I at least could see what to expect. But at the same time, knowing could be worse than going in blind. There was a reason people turned to stone when they actually looked at Medusa. Don't ever stare evil straight on.

Stay blind.

The room was silent until the sound of heels—delicate, timid—broke the asphyxiating anticipation.

Twenty young women.

I didn't know this because I was counting, but because The Order of the Silver Ghost deemed the number centuries ago.

Twenty, but only one would be mine.

Also deemed by The Order of the Silver Ghost.

As they entered the room, they stood in a line before us. You could tell by their uneasy movements that though they'd been instructed on what to do, they were still unsure if they were carrying out the steps correctly.

Long flowing ball gowns of a multitude of hues were a burst of color against the white that surrounded them. Tiny, corseted frames, massive amounts of fabrics, hand-sewn beads and diamonds—dresses that were custom made to fit each female. They were crafted princesses with the utmost beauty.

I studied the women, curious as to what they must be thinking. Some of the women would be awful poker players because their fear and nervousness was painted all over their faces. Others were impossible to read because they kept their eyes to the ground, shadowed with their own insecurities.

But there was one belle—the only one dressed in blue—who made brief eye contact with me as she measured the men who stood in front of her. I watched how she studied what we wore and how we stood. She was focused on the men rather than the massive macabre setting of the ballroom that seemed to hold the fascination of her fellow females. It was a smart move and I didn't miss the intelligence in her bright green eyes.

"Display the belles," the Elder demanded with a beat of the cane. The deep voice and the way the cane attacked the stillness caused the belles to jump or flinch. The recruits, however, remained steadfast for we were used to the sounding of the canes.

Another Elder began the procession of the belles by leading them single-file line through the ballroom. He walked them in front of the cloaked Elders first, then the members, and then to us.

They repeated the act three times, circling the room as if they were dancing around the ballroom, the only music created from the pitter patter of their shoes and the swoosh of their dresses cutting the thick air. Some smiled with too many teeth as if they were a contestant in a pageant, the lips of others trembled, and a few displayed little to no emotion at all.

The belle in blue surprised me again by making eye contact with me with each pass. Her lips remained parted, her arms by her side, her chin stayed high with a self-confidence the others seemed to lack or, at the very least, faked.

I knew each of the twenty women came from *the wrong side of the tracks*. The dresses they wore were worth more money than most would acquire in a year.

They were not Southern belles raised with etiquette coaches and groomed with rich Southern charm so coagulated it could strangle the Queen of England in heavy marmalade and sweet tea. This entire cortége was so foreign to them that I didn't hold it against any who stumbled or seemed to wobble on their heels.

But the belle in blue seemed different.

She appeared regal as she marched before us.

She stood out from the others as if she were just as much a blue blood as the color of her dress. And yet, the way she kept her shoulders back screamed resistance. Pride seemed to be the fragrance wafting from her creamy white skin. I can't say I blamed her. Who wouldn't resist this madness?

"Montgomery Kingston," the Elder called out as the women lined up once again before the recruits who hadn't moved an inch. "It is time for you to choose the belle."

The Elder who had been leading the procession of belles walked over to where I stood and opened his fist. Resting on his palm was a black satin ribbon. I needed zero instruction to know what to do next as, once again, this process was clearly laid out in our book that ruled over every breath we took.

Taking the ribbon, I took a deep inhale and stepped out from formation. I then walked up to the line of women and began what was called "the touching of the pearls". One by one, I approached each female and briefly touched the pearl necklace they all wore.

This was my time to process. To think. I had

minutes before I would have to choose, and although I was touching the smoothness of each woman's pearls, I felt nothing. Going through the motions, steadying my nerves, and focusing on the ceremonial act was all I could do. Focusing on anything else was an impossibility.

A wiser man would have taken this time to study their features, to try to pick the woman whom he had the most sexual chemistry with since in the next 109 days I would be expected to go further sexually with her than I had ever done with another. I should be picking the prettiest girl, but the truth of the matter was that they were all stunning. Again, I focused on the task at hand— following the steps I read about in the book. Just like everything in my life, I would conduct the ceremony perfectly.

And then I reached the belle in blue.

She was the first of the women who locked eyes with me as I reached out to caress her necklace. It was the first time I was close enough to see how flecks of gold danced with the color green in her eyes. The gold in her irises matched the gilded highlights in her blonde hair. Her creator had painted her beauty with an expert hand.

Long lashes hooded her gaze which softened the severity of how she stared at me, but I could see she was sizing me up just as I was her.

She never blinked... like she was daring me.

An unspoken conversation challenged me to do more than just stroke the necklace and move on like I had been doing with each girl before her.

I was the first to break the eye connection by looking down to the string of white spheres resting against her silken flesh. I picked up the necklace and placed a pearl on her glossy lower lip. I don't know what I was expecting, but the action seemed as natural as breathing.

The belle in blue parted her lips slightly, her eyes still locked on me. She didn't move, didn't cower, didn't resist.

I pushed the pearl a little further. The action between us was so subtle, and so private that I was sure the Elders wouldn't be able to make out what was happening.

It was our secret.

A clandestine act belonging to just us in a world of cloak and daggers.

Her tongue darted out and licked the pearl as a soft breath followed close behind.

Was she hushing my thoughts or blowing them away?

I circled the pearl around her tongue, coating her lips with the smoothness. The act was brief but long enough for me to know.

I wanted the belle in blue.

Not needing to continue on down the line of

other belles, I removed the pearl from her mouth and yanked hard.

The necklace broke from her neck and the tiny pearls scattered around our shoes. Her eyes widened, but she remained in place.

Breaking the necklace. An act to show just how easy it is for The Order of the Silver Ghost to give you riches only to take them away. What you believe to be yours can be ruined with such ease.

Years of pearls from broken necklaces hid in the nooks and crannies of the white ballroom. As boys, we would love sneaking into the room as our fathers conducted their meetings or met with their mistresses. We would search for the pearls and then chuck them at each other as we engaged in our own rich boy version of paint ball. Being hit with a white little bead stung like a son of a bitch, but we'd loved the game regardless.

With the only sound of the room being the rolling of pearls against the colorless floor, I replaced the white that had been on her neck with the color black. Locking eyes, I crossed the ribbon at her throat and pulled tightly. I took a moment as I yanked the satin harder and tighter than needed as a warning.

This was her chance. She could run. She could shake her head. She could give me some signal that she didn't want this. I would have given her that wish if I saw the smallest glimmer of fear. I would have moved on to a more willing belle.

But her expression never changed. Her eyes didn't flicker.

She chose me just as I chose her.

Tying the ribbon into a bow around her neck, I heard, "Montgomery Kingston, have you chosen your belle for the Initiation?"

I took a step back from the belle in blue and nodded.

"I have chosen."

Ten Minutes Earlier

Y*ou will stay calm, cool, and collected*, I told myself as they paraded us into the white ballroom, and I got my first glimpse of the silver-hooded members of The Order of the Silver Ghost.

My heart was pounding about a jillion beats per minute though I prayed it didn't show on my face. *Calm, cool, and fucking* collected. I wasn't going to let any of these men intimidate me.

At least that's what I told myself after Mrs. Hawthorne's lackeys finally finished polishing and spritzing me into perfection hours earlier.

I had still looked like myself when I was finally allowed to glance in the mirror as Mrs. Hawthorne herself lifted the string of pearls and cinched the clasp behind my neck. But it was like I was walking around with an Instagram filter on. My skin was flawless. My eyes had never seemed so large or luminous.

I thought that the pearls were just the topping on an elegant cake. When I finally met the other belles in contention for the "gentleman," that was what I was reminded of—beautiful cupcakes. We were tufted with layers of silk frosting all for the sake of being beautiful to look at. But it was an illusion. Really we were just here to be eaten up and devoured.

It was another test.

I didn't know how many would be chosen tonight, but some would go home empty-handed. How many, I also didn't know.

What I *did* know?

If I was going to go through with this, it had to be with the right man.

They paraded us in front of them, round and round, the eerie stomping of wooden canes the only noise. It felt like a pagan ceremony, a throwback to something ancient but very, very primal.

Keep your head, Grace. I just had to be analytical in my choice of a man. They thought *they* were choosing, but this was my choice, too, damn it.

I could do what they would ask of me. I hoped I could, anyway. But only with the right man. There would have to be trust. Otherwise, I didn't think I could endure three months of being mistreated and come out all right on the other side okay. What woman could?

I wanted the future I glimpsed this afternoon when I described it into the recorder. Speaking my dream out loud had made me want it more than ever.

But I wasn't so confident as to pretend I couldn't be broken.

Yes, I could only do this if I chose the right man.

My gaze was drawn to one man standing among a group of young men.

I immediately dismissed him. He was too good-looking. Jaw-droppingly handsome, actually. And okay, yeah, I stared at first. But seriously, how often do you see guys like this in real life?

His blue-gray eyes were so light, they almost went translucent when light caught them. He had casually mussed blond hair but heavy, dark eyebrows that shadowed those intense eyes. All the other men had carefully groomed and slicked-back hair, but his was stylishly unruly. Was it an act of rebellion, or was he so rich that even amongst the most elite of the elite, he was still allowed to break the rules?

Surely, he had to be a jerk. Nobody rich enough to be here and also that gorgeous could be a good guy. He never would have had any reason to be. He must've been given every single thing in life and how could a man develop compassion when he'd never known need?

I searched every other face. Mostly it was white guys, but there were some men with actual melanin there, too. From what I could see, it was the younger men wore white tuxes, and then the rest of the older men leered on from beneath their silver hoods. How many men were being initiated tonight? I couldn't tell and no one had explained the specifics of this "choosing ceremony".

Surely there'd be more than just one man for so many women to be presented tonight.

Some of the guys watched as if they were already undressing me. A few looked bored.

I tried to focus on one of the other men. There was a shy-looking one standing behind the others. He wasn't handsome but he wasn't ugly. Plain. I could handle plain.

But my gaze was pulled toward the blond Greek god. For some reason, I felt as if he had the most power. It was as if he knew he would be given first choice, the equivalent of being granted the first round draft pick, I imagined—and then there was just something in the way he stood. He had *presence*.

But then I felt *his* eyes on me.

I swear electricity tingled on my skin everywhere his gaze caressed. It was a completely inappropriate reaction for the situation. What the hell was wrong with me? This was a business deal of sorts. It was no time for... for...

"Montgomery Kingston, it is time for you to choose the belle."

The older man in the silver cloak spoke the words and yet I only had eyes for what those words evoked.

Oh my God! It couldn't be and yet it was. It was him! The man Mrs. Hawthorne had called her boy. Even his name was ostentatious: Montgomery Kingston.

It was a name that said *we have old money and you should bow at our feet.*

No, I could never allow Montgomery Kingston to be the one.

But then Montgomery started walking around each woman, caressing the identical pearls at each of their necks.

And it took everything I had to stay where I was standing and not go jerk the bitches backwards out of his grasp.

When he reached for the pearls of the belle beside me, I was close enough to hear her gasp of delight.

She wanted him. She was a pretty brunette. Catalog model pretty, not stunning. But her breasts were all but falling out the top of her gown, and I'd yet to meet a man who wouldn't choose a great rack over everything else.

Still, I watched on. Maybe even glared on.

Don't pick her. Don't pick her. Come to me.

Wait, where had that come from? Hadn't I just decided he was the one man I didn't want?

But then, with as little hesitation as he had moved on from each of the girls before her, Montgomery pulled his hand back and lifted his eyes toward me.

It was too much. I couldn't hold his gaze.

Shit. What now? Would he dismiss me just as easily as he had all the others? Was that what I wanted?

I tried to look over Montgomery's shoulder for the shy, plain guy, but Montgomery was standing right in front of me now and when I looked up, all I could see was him. Or more accurately... all I could do was stare at his lips.

He was so much taller than me, his lips were at my eye level. They were thick and full, and surrounded by the slightest stubble that made my legs quiver beneath my full skirt.

Wrong reaction. Wrong reaction! *Get your head on straight, Grace.* This man looked like a sculpted angel. But he could just as well be a devil.

Then again, there were no second chances in this dangerous game.

I sucked in a quick breath and tilted my head back so I could look Montgomery in the eye. I had about five seconds to size him up or I'd lose him. I had to look beyond his flawless face and try to see the man inside.

But I had no idea what I saw in his eyes because I...

Suddenly I couldn't think straight.

I had a plan. I was supposed to—what? What was I supposed to do? Strategize. Right, strategy was important.

I blinked but couldn't look away. The electricity buzzing between us was too loud in my ears. It drowned out every other thought.

And then he reached for my pearl necklace.

I didn't gasp only because I wasn't breathing. He lifted the pearls and placed one against my bottom lip. His blunt, calloused finger brushed the plump flesh and I opened to him. I couldn't not.

His eyes demanded and I gave.

My tongue peeked out from between my lips and his eyes darkened.

Yes. *That*. More of that. I wanted more of that. Needed it.

When he teased, playing with the pearl on my tongue, the breath I'd been holding suddenly released with a sharp expulsion.

His nostrils flared and when he suddenly pulled his hand away from my mouth, I was left weak-kneed and blinking in shock.

W-what was that? I wasn't supposed to react like this. I was supposed to be alluring and enticing, but in the way that an ice sculpture was—untouchable and cold. Not have this molten lava firing through my veins.

Our surroundings suddenly rushed back in the next moments. I was in the pristine white ballroom once again. All around us, people watched on in silence. I wasn't the only one waiting with bated breath.

And then Montgomery's hand was back on my necklace, but this time it wasn't gentle.

He tore the pearls from around my neck. The silk thread was delicate, and it snapped with only the slightest pinch. And the pearls—the beautiful, delicate pearls—they pinged to the floor like elegant little expired shell casings.

I looked to Montgomery, feeling devastation tear through my stomach.

Did I fail the test?

Was I too forward? Should I not have responded when he—

But then Montgomery was tying a black ribbon around my neck.

I didn't know what it meant. I was quickly realizing that when it came to The Order of the Silver Ghost, I knew nothing.

Dr. Nichols' words from earlier came back to me: *Don't try to anticipate. Just give in to it. There's no shame or judgment here.*

So, I didn't let myself back down. No shame. No

fear. If the black ribbon meant I was marked to be sent away, so be it.

I stood proudly. I stared Montgomery Kingston down, not giving an inch. The electricity was still there between us. I would show no fear. I'd have him or I'd have no one. It was a sudden decision, but it was the right one. I knew it to my bones.

I deserved my place here and I deserved to be *his*. He would be lucky to have me. I waited for him to realize it, too.

I saw the moment that he did. The intensity of his scrutinizing gaze eased just the tiniest bit, like a weight had been lifted from his shoulders.

And then he said the words that would seal both of our fates: "I have chosen."

His words brought a rush of elation unlike anything I'd ever felt before in my entire life. Followed by a healthy dose of fear.

Now it was time to see exactly what the hell we'd both just gotten ourselves into.

9

MONTGOMERY

I didn't even know her name.

I was about to fuck a woman within moments of "meeting" her, and I couldn't tell you a single thing about this girl other than to speak of her beauty and how she carried herself.

We were side by side, marching behind the Elders as they led us to our bedroom. I tried to remember if there were any rules on whether or not speaking was permissible before consummating the choosing.

Taking a risk, I whispered, "What's your name?" I figured if the Elders heard and it wasn't allowed, they would quickly silence me.

"Grace," she quietly replied.

"Montgomery," I said, though I was pretty sure she was aware of that fact. It still seemed like the polite thing to do.

One night stands and meaningless hookups weren't my particular taste. I actually preferred to at least know something about the women I slept with, and I often preferred to *taste* over and over again. And even though tonight wouldn't be a one-time fuck with this woman—the Order would make damn sure of it—the situation felt like one.

Cold. Emotionless. A lack of any real connection or desire to go beyond the act of sex itself.

I didn't want tonight to happen. Although, I had a feeling this was just the beginning of things I didn't want.

When we entered the spacious room on the second floor, I instantly recognized it. The truth of the matter was that I had been in all the rooms of the Oleander at one time or another playing tag or hide and go seek as a boy. Odd that I was now entering as a man about to begin my Initiation.

This room was by far one of the largest and even had its own fireplace. The large king size, four-post canopy bed barely filled the massive space. There was plenty of room for a sitting area with a small couch and two high-back armchairs that sat before the handcrafted mantle.

The large window with flowing drapes over-looked the pool and rose gardens of the expansive grounds. The room had colorful rugs, rich-toned wood furniture, collectible books in a custom-made bookcase, and antiques dating from the Civil War era.

My favorite part of the room had always been the bedspread that simply screamed The Order of the Silver Ghost. It was rich-toned silver that matched the cloaks the members wore with gold embroidery hand sewn by a seamstress long past. Rumor was that the gold thread used was actually made from treasures plundered in the medieval days of battles fought and won. I never imagined that I would not only be sleeping under the fabric but having sex on it.

I hadn't looked at Grace fully since leaving the ballroom other than a quick glance here and there out of the corner of my eye. Side by side we stood as the Elders gathered at the foot of the bed, and I knew the poor girl had to be terrified. How could she not be? But I wanted to see for myself and stole a full look upon her face.

If she was afraid, she hid it well.

Stoic beauty.

I knew what to expect as the Order clearly spelled this ritual out in our society's handbook. I knew every step that would occur, and I wasn't sure if it was a blessing or a curse that Grace had no real idea what was coming.

The first beat of the cane announced it was time for the consummation to begin.

Silver cloaks, beady eyes, and fucked up appetites stared upon the empty bed waiting...

There would be no privacy.

Prolonging the inevitable would only torture us both, so I took hold of Grace's shoulders and turned her to face me. I would offer her one last chance to give me any signal to stop. Show me distress and I would walk her out of the Manor myself. This was her chance to use her safe word, to cry, to snap some sense into herself, to do anything but go down this twisted path.

But the stoic beauty remained.

I had no choice but to continue on.

Step one: strip the belle naked.

Tonight would not be about the art of seduction. Taking it slow would not benefit either one of us as we had a line of men watching our every move.

Taking hold of her blue gown, I began its removal as if I were a robot. I didn't want to concentrate on the how but more the chore of it. It was just a step. The first step. Get her naked and we could just get this over with and the Elders would leave us alone.

The quiet of the room was maddening, and I needed to move fast. Grace stood in place with her arms at her side. It was clear she wasn't going to fight me, but she sure as hell wasn't going to help me, and I didn't blame her one bit.

As the dress pooled at her feet, I couldn't help but admire the lingerie-clad woman before me. I would be lying if I said my body didn't react to the sight. I also would be lying if I didn't also feel some relief when my cock hardened because I had actually considered stealing a blue pill from my father's medicine cabinet to help me get through this night but couldn't bring myself to do so. The last thing I needed was performance issues to occur as I fucked—or tried to fuck—in front of the Elders during my Initiation. I'd had no idea if my body would revolt or respond.

Clearly, as my pants tented, my body chose to respond regardless of the fucked up voyeuristic situation I was in.

I could have stared upon her longer. I could have lowered my lips to the lace of her panties and her bra and licked along the edges as I wanted to do, but this was not the time. There may never be the time, but I knew that this very moment was most definitely not it.

Finishing step one, I divested her of the sexy undergarments, taking a step back and inhaling deeply to steady my nerves. Her entire body was now on full display before me. The only thing she wore was the black ribbon I had tied around her neck. She was my package. A dark gift. Mine.

It was a moment that wouldn't last long. The Elders still looked upon the empty bed waiting, and so for this short time, Grace was only mine to gaze upon. Only I got to watch as she stood at attention before me. Perky breasts that would fill my palms, curves in all the right places, and a bare pussy just begging to be devoured.

Her eyes were hooded by thick lashes, and her lip quivered. I could see it, sense it... she was fighting against the shame.

I wouldn't have any part of that. I needed to take the burden of shame off her shoulders if possible.

If she was naked, I would be too.

I didn't have to remove all my clothing. Nowhere in the handbook did it say I had to be naked. I could have just taken my pants down and shoved my dick inside of her as I'm sure many recruits had done in the past, but I was not that man.

I owed her more.

She deserved equal.

If she was bare and exposed, I sure as fuck would be too.

And besides, there was a sick side of me that wanted those old fucks who would be watching to have to see my bare ass. Make them feel awkward —and most certainly envious—as they stared upon my dick that no doubt was much larger than any of theirs. I was proud of my lean, toned, and muscular body and would use it to my advantage to play mind games with the men who were forced to watch me fuck like they could only fantasize of doing as they stroked their limp and wrinkled cocks while watching porn.

Step two: bend her over the bed and claim from behind.

The good thing about fucking her in this position was that I wouldn't have to see her face. I wouldn't feel her breath on my mouth tempting me to kiss her as I entered her. I wouldn't have to feel her body in my arms or hold her close in an intimate way I knew neither of us wanted or even expected.

This wasn't making love. It was sex in the most raw, primal and depraved way while others watched. We might as well fuck like animals since we were practically in a cage surrounded by our keepers.

I took hold of her arms and led her to the edge of the bed. She didn't resist or even tense up. In fact, she was the one who bent over and placed her palms on the silver and gold bed covering.

And thank God for that, because there was a split moment I froze and nearly buckled at the knees as she did so. I shouldn't have glanced over to the Elders. I shouldn't have looked.

Motherfucker!

I knew he would be there. Deep down I knew. Of course he would be there. He was an Elder. But

I didn't want to see his face, his judging eyes, his lips with a wicked smirk. I didn't want to actually see him!

My father.

My father would watch me as I fucked this woman.

Sick, disgusting, twisted, and I had no choice but to quickly close my eyes and force the image out of my mind. I had to block the vision of him watching. I had to. I had to. He would not break me, and if I failed to fuck this woman... I would fail on the first night.

No, Dad, no. You will not win. So, watch all you want. Watch me do it better than you ever could. Watch me. I will complete every single step of this Initiation, and there is nothing you can do to stop me. Watch, motherfucker. Watch.

Her ass. Yes, focus on her ass because as it was bent over the bed, it had the power to fully captivate my entire attention. Creamy white called to me. Her thin thighs were sealed tightly together, but I knew she would allow me to breach the connection for we had already crossed the line of no return. But regardless, I wanted more.

I stepped up behind her and pressed my hard cock at the seam of her ass. Bending over her positioned form, I placed my lips at her ear, wrapped my arm around her body, and I caressed her pussy searching for her clit.

When I made contact with my destination, and I felt her body tense beneath me, I circled and applied pressure to hopefully wake up a sexual need that could very well be ice cold.

With my lips still at her ear, I whispered, "Say yes. I need to hear it. Say yes."

I heard her gasp and decided to lower my hand to her entrance and coated my finger in her wetness. I wouldn't penetrate... not yet.

"Say it," I demanded again. Maybe the Elders could hear. Maybe not. I didn't care.

My finger waited. I waited. But I wanted to press inside of her so badly that my cock throbbed in anticipation.

"Yes," she finally whispered. "Yes," she repeated in case I didn't hear.

Not with ease, but with force, I shoved my finger deep inside of her. Pumping in and out, I took pride in the fact that her pussy got wetter with every movement. I refused to fuck a dry pussy. She deserved better than that. We both did.

She remained quiet, but I could hear how her breathing changed when I added a second finger to ready her body for my size. Her body trembled beneath mine as I inched my cock closer to her hole as it awaited its turn.

Step three: consummate the union.

With no control left inside of me, I guided the head of my cock to her entrance. Taking hold of her hips with my hands, I thrust deep inside of her. She was so damn tight that a groan escaped my lips which was the cue the Elders were waiting for.

The beating of the canes began.

Over and over, a rhythmic cadence set the pace. The sound of the canes seemed to control my speed as I fucked the woman beneath me.

In and out, beat after beat.

She bucked against me, meeting my cock with every push, forcing me to go deeper inside of her. My balls slapped against her firm ass, and I worried I wouldn't last long.

Our bodies danced to the haunting staccato. I watched as her fingers clawed at the mattress as she arched her back in what I could only assume to be signs of pleasure.

The canes seemed to hypnotize our bodies, and the hungry stares of the Elders acted as a catalyst to our performance. We fucked for others, but we fucked for ourselves at the same time.

Her moans met mine, and I rewarded our animalistic need for completion by driving in and out faster and with more force. The canes pounded against the floor at my pace, matching every thrust.

In and out.

Beat after beat.

I was ready to cum, to fill her tight little hole with my seed, but I was determined to give her a release first. Her pussy milked my cock, and I knew how close she was.

Reaching around her again, I put my finger on her clit and demanded completion. With nothing but a quick touch, her moans turned to a mewl, and her body shook beneath me.

It was all I needed to explode inside her as my moans were muffled by the loud pounding of the canes.

I could hear nothing but the hammering caused by the Elders in a chaotic level of madness. There was no order or rhythm like before, but instead a cacophony that surrounded our completion of the consummation.

I remained in place to catch my breath, as did Grace. We waited. We listened. We froze connected while we waited for the canes to stop.

And then there was silence.

With my dick still inside the stranger beneath me, I glanced over to the Elders once more as they turned to march out of the room. My eyes connected with my father's once again, but this time...

It was *me* who gave the wicked smirk.

With one final beat of their canes, the Elders of The Order of the Silver Ghost exited the room.

The next morning, Mrs. Hawthorne unceremoniously dropped a tray full of food in front of me before returning to the sideboard and then taking Montgomery's tray to the opposite end of the long table. And I do mean a *very* long table. Comically long if Montgomery and I were supposed to attempt any conversation from one end to the other.

Or maybe the point was to give us some distance after our all-too-close encounter last night. I swallowed hard and started fanning myself. Couldn't we turn the fan on or something? I'd felt fevered ever since waking up beside Montgomery this morning.

"Here's your breakfast, laddie."

I could only watch on in shock as Mrs. Hawthorne's face softened—something I didn't know it was capable of—when she set Montgomery's tray in front of him. His food had a silver dome on top that mine hadn't. Mrs. Hawthorne pulled it off with a flourish, patting Montgomery on the back and beaming down at him. "All your favorites."

"Thanks, Mrs. H," he said, not looking up from the newspaper he was apparently absorbed in.

He'd been like this ever since we'd woken up together. Well, since *I'd* woken up anyway. When I'd finally blinked awake in his sumptuous bed, he'd already been dressed in a suit and starched shirt, sitting in a side chair by the large window reading the newspaper.

Both of our phones had been taken away for the duration of the trial, so we only had old-school access to the outside world apart from his work laptop.

I'd pulled the sheets around myself, shy for some ridiculous reason in spite of all we'd done together last night. He'd been... *inside* me. I'd had sex before but it was nothing, and I mean, *nothing* like that. He was so... so powerful and commanding but gentle and considerate at the same time. He could've just done a quick couple thrusts and cum to satisfy the Elders, but he'd readied me and brought me with him until I was a quivering, shuddering ball of need beneath him.

"Hi," I'd ventured quietly.

I wasn't sure what I expected, but it was more than his curt, "Get dressed. We'll be late for breakfast if you don't hurry."

That was it. Two sentences from the man who had known my body so intimately last night.

I scurried into action, though. Everything was a test, right? I didn't want to fail on my first day.

So, I quickly showered and got ready. By the time I came out of the bathroom in my towel, a day dress was laid out on the bed for me, along with fresh underthings. I grabbed them and scurried back into the bathroom to change.

When I came back out, Montgomery had the paper folded underneath his elbow. He held out his opposite arm to me. "Shall we?"

It was such a gentlemanly gesture, but there was something off about his voice. He was being weirdly distant, and I didn't understand why. Had I done something wrong? I couldn't imagine what it could have been.

Still, I decided to just go with the flow. I took his arm, and he led me down the long hallway, down the grand staircase, to a room with a table that had to be over fifteen feet long. He deposited me at one end and then went all the way to the opposite end where he sat now.

I had to squint to make out his facial features, we were seated so far apart, and that was only if I ducked to look around the enormous flower arrangements set up as a centerpiece in the middle of the table. Not to mention the fact that as soon as he got settled in, he shook out the paper and lifted it in front of his face like a shield between us.

I could only stare at my surroundings.

The dining room was something out of a magazine. The dark mahogany table was waxed and shined to perfection even though it had to be almost as old as the house. Luxurious valances covered the tops of the windows, but the heavier curtains were tied off at the sides, revealing a lighter white curtain that let in more light and billowed in the mid-morning wind.

I appreciated the fresh air and tried to draw as much of it into my lungs as possible, at the same time I dug my toes into the sumptuous rug below. *Stay calm and collected.* Last night wasn't so bad. Parts of it had even been... unexpectedly very nice. My cheeks blushed hot remembering shuddering in Montgomery's arms as I came.

Montgomery acted like he sat among this sort of opulence every morning. Maybe he did. Maybe this was an ordinary Saturday morning for him.

My breakfast usually consisted of grabbing a Pop-Tart on my way out the door because I was running late for my 7 a.m. shift at the diner. We didn't bother having a dining room table in our trailer because space was tight, and we always ate on the couch while watching TV anyway. Yep, we were that classy.

Ten minutes later, Mrs. Hawthorne was coming in with our food.

I stared down at the halved grapefruit and eggs in tiny little cups the exact size and shape to hold them. But they still had their shells, so how exactly were you supposed to eat the eggs?

I watched on in fascination as Montgomery picked up one of the several spoons laid out beside his napkin. He tapped the egg, then expertly peeled off the top and began to eat the soft-boiled egg within.

But when I tried to repeat the action, all I managed to do was make a web-like fracture in the egg's shell. I tried again and the whole side of the egg smooshed in. I immediately set the spoon down and pushed the little egg out of the way.

Grapefruit, that I knew how to eat.

Except that I hated grapefruit. It was too sour.

Montgomery grabbed a second spoon and ate the fruit elegantly out of its rind.

Maybe I should give grapefruit a second chance. It might be sweeter than I remembered. I valiantly speared some with my spoon, but apparently I did so too vigorously, because juice squirted all over the front of my dress. I couldn't help my little yelp of surprise, which finally made Montgomery look at me.

"Sorry," I cringed, holding up my spoonful of grapefruit. "Juicy little suckers, huh?"

I wasn't sure because I was so far away from him, but I thought I saw a smirk to the side of his lips. He went back to his paper a second later and I rolled my eyes and shoved the grapefruit in my mouth.

Only to choke on it. Blech. Ugh! So sour! I managed to swallow the bite but couldn't help the way my face contorted at the sour flavor.

I immediately grabbed the closest cup I could and chugged it, looking for some relief. Too bad the cup I grabbed was what I thought was orange-juice. But when the juice hit my tongue, it only made the sourness worse.

Dear God, had they mixed the orange-juice with grapefruit juice, too? Who were these sadistic bastards?

I barely managed to keep myself from spitting it out, but I couldn't help choking and coughing as soon as I swallowed it down. Some of it went down the wrong pipe, too, so I was coughing even harder.

And then suddenly Montgomery was there, his firm hand pounding my back. "Are you okay? Just try to take a deep breath."

I knew my face must be as red as a lobster as I gasped for breath. Oh yeah, I was the absolute picture of elegance right now. Facepalm.

My eyes watered as I pushed my chair back

from the table and doubled over, trying to catch my breath. That only made me cough harder. Montgomery continued to rub my back and then he magically produced a cup of ice water. I grabbed for it and sipped the cool water, coughing a few more times before finally catching my breath.

"Thanks," I finally managed to croak, looking up at Montgomery through wet lashes. Dear God, I must look like a mess. If this breakfast was a test, I just failed dismally.

"You're welcome. Here." He handed me a white cloth napkin and I swiped at my face, cringing at the mascara that came away on the crisp white linen. I swiped underneath my eyes, hoping to minimize the damage.

"I guess I'm a failure at this elegant lady stuff, huh?" My smile was wobbly as I looked up at Montgomery.

He frowned briefly. "You're doing just fine."

He pulled back and looked like he was about to go back to his end of the table, but I reached out and clasped my small hand around his wrist. "Wait," I whispered. "Don't go."

He looked surprised by my request.

"I just mean, can't we talk a little? I'm not really sure what happens now. What happens next, I mean. Will it always be like last night? Them all... watching us like that?"

I couldn't keep holding his gaze while I remembered everything from last night. I dropped my eyes back to the table, but I didn't let go of his wrist. The next second, though, he pulled it away out of my grasp.

"No. It'll be different."

I looked back at him, startled. "What do you mean?"

He sighed and ran a hand through his hair. "I thought they would've told you more to prepare you."

"They didn't."

His jaw flexed as he looked out the window. "I'm beginning to see that."

I stayed quiet, waiting for him to continue.

After a short silence, he did, but he kept looking out the window, not at me. "It'll be different. Invitations will continue to come for events of different kinds. We'll continue to be asked to"—his eyes flicked my way, but only briefly—"to *perform*. Like we did last night."

Perform. Perform *sex*.

I blinked and looked down at the table.

"What's my safeword?" We hadn't talked about it last night. There really hadn't been time.

Montgomery looked surprised by my question. "It's whatever you want it to be."

"Pearl necklace."

He barked out a laugh, and I felt my chest go warm.

A noise from behind us had me looking over my shoulder. There were footsteps on the stairs. Montgomery shifted beside me, and I knew he was looking too.

It was one of the women from last night. Another one of the prospective belles. And she was obviously doing the walk of shame, barefoot, her hair disheveled, and still wearing her ballgown from the night before. Beside her was a tall, thin man with short gray hair.

He looked in our direction and smiled. It wasn't directed at me, though. He smiled at Montgomery, and I felt Montgomery go ramrod stiff beside me.

"Father," Montgomery clipped out.

The girl looked our direction, her mouth dropping open before she scurried down the last few stairs. But Montgomery's father jogged the last few steps, caught her around the elbow, and kissed her deeply, reaching a hand around and spanking her ass until she yelped and giggled.

When he finally pulled away from the girl, he stared straight at Montgomery, giving the girl's breast a last squeeze before sending her on her way.

I thought he might approach us, but he just smirked and followed the girl out.

I didn't like that man. Montgomery's father. I looked to Montgomery and saw his jaw was tight again, but I had no idea what he was thinking.

"I don't understand," I said quietly after the front door slammed behind them. "That girl. I thought we could only be claimed by initiates."

"Sometimes the discarded girls think sleeping with the Elders is still a ticket to a better life."

"Is it?"

Montgomery glared at me. "Only if you think being a part-time whore who occasionally gets rewarded with diamond bracelets or other trinkets is a life you want."

His words were vehement and full of anger, maybe even hatred. I didn't understand him. Did he hate me? Did he think I was a whore? I was essentially sleeping with him for money.

"Why did you choose me?" The question was out of my mouth before I really thought about it.

It was the wrong thing to ask, I could tell by the way Montgomery's face immediately shut down. His features became even more severe as he turned to me.

"Don't get any romantic notions in your head. We both want something and these trials will help us achieve those goals. We're here to use each other to get ahead. Nothing more."

His words felt like a slap across the face.

"Who said I have any romantic notions?" Outrage out of proportion to the situation lit through me, and I had no idea why.

But I'd never been good at holding my tongue.

"You think just because you're rich and a little bit handsome every woman in a fifty-mile radius wants to fall down at your feet and fawn all over you like Mrs. Hawthorne does? Ha." I sat up straighter in my chair. "I just thought we could be civil to each other since we're in this together."

"We aren't in this together. We're in this separately. I get what I want. You get what you want. End of story."

"Fine." I lifted my chin a notch higher. "Then tell me the rules so I don't incur your anger, oh master."

His eyes narrowed on me. "You aren't to go anywhere alone in the mansion without me escorting you. You will watch your tongue. You will understand that for the next three plus months, you're in a world where women are silent and men rule. I don't care if you don't like it. No one is forcing you to be here. So, either use your safe word and lose everything, or do what you're told."

"Because you want to use me like a sex toy just like your father used that woman?"

Well, that set him off.

"*Never*. I'm nothing like my father." The words came out hissed through his teeth, and he'd advanced so that his face was only inches from mine.

"Why are you doing all of this if you hate it so

much?" I asked. I genuinely didn't understand him. "Why are you here?"

"I'm here because this is just the way things are. I'm here to get what's owed me. Now, I don't see any reason for further discussion between us. We're here to do a job, and we'll do it. That's the end of it."

It was my turn to glare at him. That was the end of it? Just because he declared it was? What a pretentious, overstuffed, overbearing—

A bell rang and then Mrs. Hawthorne reentered the room carrying another tray. She came in smiling but then saw Montgomery and me facing off. Her smile immediately turned into a glare, directed straight at me.

"Are you disrupting the peace on your first morning, girl?" she snapped.

I threw my hands up in the air. "I didn't do anything!"

"Everything's fine, Mrs. H. Is our second course ready?"

Her face softened again. "Yes. I've also been instructed by your father to deliver the invitations for tonight's event."

Montgomery took the tray from Mrs. Hawthorne. "Thanks, Mrs. H. I'll take it from here."

Mrs. Hawthorne fussed at him. "That's not your job, laddie. I'm here to take care of you."

Montgomery smiled at her, again showing the

tenderness that I sometimes glimpsed in him. Which only made his coldness to me more frustrating and confusing. "You've taken care of me for years. Why don't you take the morning off?"

"I've never taken a morning off in all the years I've worked here!" Mrs. Hawthorne sounded offended at the mere suggestion, her accent thicker than ever in her ire.

But Montgomery was busy looking down at the thick, cream-colored invitation he'd picked up from the tray after he set it on the long table.

He handed me a second invitation. "I'll take you back to the room. I have things to attend to today, so you can finish your meal there and prepare yourself for the evening activities."

I took the invitation with only the slightest hesitation, hastily reading to see what tonight would have in store for me.

At the bottom were instructions: *You will serve your master at his feet all night long as his obedient pet.*

11

MONTGOMERY

I wondered what would be worse. The Initiations or waiting for them. Killing time in awkward silence in our prison cell was far from easy. The tick of the clock that sat on the bedside table as each second passed had me fighting the urge to throw it against the wall.

Grace seemed to be handling everything all right as she spent most of the day curled up in a chair reading a book.

I busied myself with my laptop trying to keep up with work. I was glad I had decided to check in because my father was already stepping in and trying to take over deals and projects that I was overseeing.

I needed to mark my territory and make sure that the staff knew that though I would be out of the office for 109 days, I was still around. And since it was just a matter of time until the business would be mine fully, they would be wise to not overstep or allow my father to control them. This would be a good time to truly see who I would be able to trust or not when this entire process was over.

A tray of meats and cheese had been brought to us for lunch, and since we had a bathroom connected to our room, we really had no reason to leave the room yet. I think we were both grateful to have some quiet time to be alone with our thoughts and just mentally prepare for whatever the night would bring us.

We both nearly jumped from our seats when there was a knock on the door and Mrs. H entered the room with two boxes in her arms.

"I have your attire for the night," she said, looking at me with a smile and walking past Grace as if she didn't exist.

"Thank you, Mrs. H," I said for both Grace and myself since I figured Grace would remain quiet.

Mrs. H shot a quick look at Grace and then focused her attention back on me. "Good luck tonight." She quickly left the room without saying another word.

"I don't know why that woman hates me," Grace said as she closed her book and placed it on the table beside her.

"That's just Mrs. H. It takes her a while to warm up to people. You have to remember that I've known her my entire life."

Grace stood up and walked over to the boxes that Mrs. H had placed on the bed. "I wonder what expensive gown and jewels they have planned for me tonight."

I fought the urge to laugh and had to also try not to smile. I had a feeling Grace was about to lose her mind, and I couldn't help but find the coming surprise to be hilarious... in a very dark and twisted way.

I must have not done as good of a job as I hoped hiding my amusement.

"What?" she asked. "What's so funny?"

I simply shook my head and waited for her to open her box. I didn't know exactly what would be inside of it, but I had a pretty good idea.

As she opened the box, her wide eyes and her, "What the fuck?" had me bursting into laughter.

She pulled out a black collar and a gold leash. Her mouth was wide open, and her fingers held her evening's attire like they were on fire.

She looked at me with stunned horror. "Is this some kind of joke?"

I kept laughing and shook my head.

"Why are you laughing?" she shouted. "They can't seriously expect me to wear this? And where is the actual clothing?" She looked back inside the box as if hoping to have missed something. "They want me to be naked? Are you fucking kidding me!"

My belly hurt from laughing. I was such a cruel bastard, but her reaction was priceless, and I had a really sick sense of humor.

She tossed the collar and leash onto the bed and yanked open my box. "And what do you have to wear tonight?" When she pulled out a black tuxedo, bowtie, and polished black shoes, she rolled her eyes. "I can't believe this shit. You get to dress up, and I have to be a... what... a dog? A naked dog?"

"You didn't expect this to be easy, now did you?" I asked, finally able to stop laughing. "And it's not like you haven't been naked in front of the Order before."

"But not at a dinner! Am I supposed to just eat my dry chicken, fumble with my too many forks, and try to be a well-mannered lady all with my bare ass on full display?"

"If that is what they have planned for the evening, then yes."

She picked up the collar and leash again. "What if I refuse?"

My face grew serious. "You know the answer to that question."

She huffed. "I can't believe I'm even considering this."

"It could be worse," I offered.

"How?"

"The leash could have to come out of your ass rather than from around your neck."

Her green eyes nearly popped out of her head. "You all are sick fucks, you know that?"

I started to laugh again. "Guilty. And, my dear, you haven't seen anything yet."

Without saying another word, Grace took her leash and collar and stormed to the bathroom. I knew she would go through with the night—in fact, I was pretty convinced she would go through with the entire Initiation. I could see she was a determined woman who would refuse to fail or allow the "sick fucks" to get one over on her, and I admired her even more for it.

I quickly changed into my tux while waiting for Grace to come out of the bathroom. For a woman who had next to nothing to get dressed in, she was taking an awfully long time.

I walked to the closed door and knocked. "Grace? Is everything all right?"

"Yes," her muffled voice answered.

"We need to get going so we aren't late. Do you need any help?"

"Yes." I heard a click as she unlocked the door, and a crack opened. She stood with a towel wrapped around her body, her hair hung loose with the tumbling blonde waves cascading down her back, and red lips. "I can't fasten the collar behind my neck."

I took the collar and the leash and fastened it while I looked at her reflection in the mirror. She was stunning. No one could deny that fact, and though I had never desired a woman at my feet in a collar before, I could suddenly see the appeal with Grace doing it.

And those lips.

My cock twitched at the thought of them wrapped around me as she sucked and licked.

My sinful thoughts were broken when I noticed how tightly she clung to the towel around her. We wouldn't be able to leave the room with her wearing it, but I also understood that her simply dropping the towel and acting like all was normal as she wore nothing but a collar with a leash attached was an impossibility as well.

I removed my tux jacket and wrapped it around her shoulders. I then took hold of the towel and pulled it off of her so she wouldn't have to force herself to drum up the courage to do it herself.

Looking her directly in the eyes through the mirror's reflection, I said, "We need to go."

She nodded and secured the jacket around herself. It was big enough and long enough that it covered most of her body, and though she wouldn't be able to keep it on for the dinner, it would at least get us down the hall and stairs, offering her some amount of dignity.

When we approached the door to the room hosting the dinner, I paused, removed the jacket, and shrugged back into it myself. I placed my hand on Grace's shoulder and pushed down firmly.

"You need to get on all fours," I said low enough that only she and I could hear the command.

She didn't resist, but instead bent down on hands and knees and waited for me to take control. Her ass was firm, her body poised for attack like a cougar, and I felt the overwhelming need to reach down and stroke her smooth skin.

I also had the urge to slap that bare ass as a kinky lust surged through my veins.

Delicious... and though I wasn't hungry for dinner, I sure as fuck was ravenous for her.

I would have to try to keep my eyes from looking at her through the evening if I was going to be able to control myself. Having a woman in a collar at my feet had never been a kink of mine, but watching Grace... a new flame emerged from the shadows of my dark desires begging to be ignited.

With the leash tightly gripped, I opened the door and entered the room. The Elders and members all stood around the room with drinks in hand, chatting as if this were any normal business dinner party.

No one wore cloaks. They were just dressed in expensive tuxedos and donned even more expensive watches and cufflinks. Power and wealth dominated the air space.

It would all seem normal except for one major detail. All around the room, women were kneeling at their feet wearing nothing but a collar and a leash just as Grace was now doing.

Our pets.

At least Grace wouldn't be alone in her nudity with all eyes on her. I hoped she felt the same, and in some crazy way prayed this scene before us gave her some sort of comfort.

"Our guest of honor has arrived," Mr. St. Claire announced. He held up his glass of scotch in my direction. "Gentlemen, shall we?" He pointed to the long table with dinner settings already in place. Massive candelabras were the only centerpieces casting a gothic element to what would otherwise be a presentation fitting for a room full of billionaires.

Gold engraved place cards were at each seat, but I already knew I would be at the end of the table facing my father at the head. Someday I would be at the head, and I had to remind myself of that as I tugged on the leash to lead a crawling Grace toward my seat. Walking slowly for her sake, knowing the marble floor on her palms and knees had to be cold and bruising, I kept my eyes focused ahead.

Not all the men were as considerate as me, however. Some of the Elders tugged their pets hard, nearly dragging them behind their fast stride. Other women seemed to know exactly what to do and handled themselves with an elegant aura. This wasn't their first dinner party at The Oleander apparently.

My father, being the asshole he was, actually took hold of his pet's hair rather than the leash and led her to the table as she grimaced and hissed in pain. I actually hoped that Grace saw the rough handling of the pets just so she could witness the comparison.

Yes, she no doubt considered me to be a monster. But I wanted her to see just how much more of a beast I could be.

When I took my seat, and Grace knelt at my feet, taking her cue from what the other pets did, I reached down and caressed the top of her head. My action wasn't to demean, but to silently compliment her on how well she had done up to this point. We were on the same side, and I needed to remind her of that for this Initiation to continue through its entire duration.

The first course was delivered, and my father used it as a cue to truly begin the dinner. "Our food has arrived," he said with the same smile I recognized from the consummation. Interesting that I had known this man my entire life and don't remember him ever looking this way. "Let's feed our hunger, gentlemen."

He reached below the table as did all the men. Pants were unzipped, some members lifted their asses enough out of their seats so they could pull down their pants, while others simply freed their cocks from the restraints of their zippers. My father looked at me and nodded, making it clear I was to do the same.

Were we going to sit around this table with our dicks out as we ate dinner?

But then the question was answered for me when I saw and heard the shuffling of knees as the pets all positioned themselves at their master's ready sex and began to suck them off. The pets who were clearly not as experienced, such as Grace, all hesitated at first, but eventually did the same.

Even Grace...

I could see her eyes scan the women as Grace observed the others engage in this wicked act. I watched as she took a deep breath and licked her lips. She didn't wait long, but instead mimicked the others and crawled between my legs.

Looking up at me with her big green eyes, she lowered her painted red lips and kissed the tip of my hard cock as an announcement of what was about to occur.

Men moaned, others ate their clam chowder while their dicks were sucked, some chatted casually with their neighbors as if there wasn't a woman giving them a blow job under the table. I could do nothing more but to take hold of Grace's hair with both my hands and help guide her head all the way to the base. I made her take all of me right from the start.

No teasing. No easing. All of me.

She grasped my cock with her thin fingers and stroked me as she tightly pulled her lips up my length while licking a path the entire way. Up and down, she began to bob. Her tongue circled, her fist tightened, her mouth caressed, and I moaned with zero shame as I blocked out the dinner guests around me.

It was just me and Grace.

Her mouth. My cock.

So right, even though it was so wrong.

"Our pets need their milk, gentlemen. It's only fair they feast too," I heard my father say, but quickly directed all my attention back toward Grace and how she mastered my body with the way she worshiped my dick.

When she opened her mouth a little wider and nearly swallowed my cock, I felt my control wavering. I refused to give this kitty her milk on her terms.

They would be on mine. Always mine.

I tightened my grip on her hair and took control of the cadence as I fucked her face. Up and down, fast and hard, and with me in the driver's seat.

Yes, I was taught to be a gentleman, but when it came to sex, I was the one who would dominate always. I would cum in her mouth, but not yet. I needed to savor the beautiful sight before me a little longer.

Moans grew in intensity, guttural groans of completion surrounded me, and I could see women fall back on their haunches wiping the remnants of their master's seed from their lips.

But I wasn't ready yet. Not yet.

I knew I was pushing Grace to the limit with how much she could take. I shoved my cock deeper with each thrust, and though her eyes watered, and her mascara began to run down her perfect hollowed cheeks, she didn't resist in the slightest.

Her eyes locked with mine as if daring me to do more.

Push harder.

Claim her mouth as I had claimed her pussy less than twenty-four hours earlier.

The second course came even though I hadn't

yet touched the first. But it didn't matter. My hunger was being satisfied in a much better way.

My Grace.

Mine.

Not being able to take it any longer, and as she lowered all the way to the base once more, I spilled my seed in the back of her throat. My ears rang, my toes curled, and I couldn't remember the last time I orgasmed with such intensity. Grace paused as she swallowed around my dick and then gently pulled away, seductively looking up at me as she wiped at her mouth and smiled.

She fucking smiled.

It was right then and there that I knew I had my perfect belle. She would be just fine in this entire process. They wouldn't be able to break her.

Oh, how they would try.

But they would never be able to break this belle.

12

After the scene at the dinner party, I think we both needed to take a step back and catch our breath. Everything just got so intense, so fast.

And then I was naked at his feet, sucking him down my throat. But for the first time in my life, the act hadn't felt like a "job" in spite of its name.

It was the craziest, most out-of-control situation, even though everybody was sitting there so calmly. Around us, they just all dined off their fine china as if nothing was amiss, silverware and champagne glasses clinking.

Meanwhile, us girls were on the floor between their legs...

I could feel Montgomery's every response in the flex of his thighs. My ministrations were killing him but still he fought release. I don't know why it turned me on as much as it did. Giving head usually felt like tiresome work, but the way he caressed my head with a mixture of tenderness and dominance... it *connected* to something inside me.

So, I just stopped thinking. Stopped judging myself for what I thought should or shouldn't be my reaction in the situation. And I gave in to it. Gave in to him as he stared down at me with those stern but fiery eyes of his.

But later, as we got ready for bed, all that had been open and laid bare at dinner was suddenly yanked back again. Montgomery retreated inside himself, and he stayed there all week. Even though we shared a room, we might as well have been on different continents.

There was only one large bed, but Montgomery took some extra towels and a blanket to make a bed roll on the floor beside the bay window. He slept there all week long.

And though he'd displayed unapologetic dominance over me in front of the other men at each event, in private, he was deferential and quiet. He'd silently hold the door open for me if he saw that I was heading to the restroom.

He cleaned up his bed roll every morning and helped make the bed even though he never slept in it.

All day long, he worked diligently on his laptop at the small table in the corner while I spent my days reading. He seemed busy and important and I wanted to ask him about a billion questions about his life and what he did for a living.

But there was a line between us. I didn't know who had laid it down, though really, I guess that wasn't true. It was him.

He'd put these boundaries in place, but I couldn't say I wasn't grateful for them. With every over-complicated dish that arrived each meal, I realized more and more that I was out of my depth here.

Montgomery was a breed of a different kind and that was the point—he'd been *bred* to be this way. This was a small group of people whose bloodlines had been fostered, and in their flawed minds *perfected*, over generations with traditions and rituals that were almost as sacred as church. Maybe even more so, because their power and money made them gods in this kingdom on earth.

So yes, it was best if I didn't mix too much with Montgomery's kind. The aura of distant politeness we'd created over the past seven days suited me *juuuuuuuuust* fine.

Except for one *tiny* problem.

Every so often, I'd catch Montgomery's head *not* bent over his work. Every so often, I'd catch him looking at me.

And okay, maybe sometimes, just sometimes... when I caught him looking? He was catching me back, because I was already looking at him.

Gah! Everything would be perfect if it weren't for that damned buzz of electricity between us.

He might not be in the bed with me, but sometimes I still couldn't sleep for knowing his hot, masculine body was only feet away from.

No matter how loud the crickets were outside, I could always hear his breathing. The way it settled out when he finally fell asleep. He didn't snore like some of my boyfriends had in the past. It was more of a regular, loud-but-still-soothing exhale, like every ten seconds he was finally releasing tension he'd been carrying around with him all during the daytime with each heavy expulsion of breath.

Sometimes I wondered if he'd breathe easier if I were sleeping next to him. I wondered if he'd ever had anybody totally on his side, one hundred percent with no conflicts of interest. It seemed like a pretty convoluted, cutthroat world he lived in. Was there anyone he could actually trust?

And then I reminded myself it was none of my business.

I'd part ways with this gorgeous man who carried the world on his shoulders and a wicked dominant streak in his eyes when he got the hankering, and I wouldn't look back. There were a thousand reasons why I couldn't afford to.

I was just reaffirming this decision when another invitation came with our lunch. Gingerapple chicken salad on a crisp bed of greens... and an invitation accompanied by another box.

My stomach flipped when I saw how small the box was. It wasn't much bigger than last week's, and surely it wasn't big enough to contain much actual clothing.

"Thank you, Mrs. H," Montgomery said to Mrs. Hawthorne. She beamed at him and then headed back out the door, closing it behind her.

I looked up at Montgomery for a second and got startled when our eyes met. Especially when the smirk I hadn't seen all week suddenly came back, tipping up one side of his mouth.

"Ready to be outraged?" he teased.

I should've been mad, but seeing this completely different side of Montgomery all of a sudden had me feeling ridiculous. I swiped the box out of his hands and opened it.

"I don't get it," I said, looking down at the three differently colored collars in the white box. They were all made of leather. One was black, one was red, and one was white. I hadn't expected clothes, though I had maybe hoped for at least some underwear. But I didn't know what to make of this. Was I supposed to wear all three, on like, different parts of my body, or what?

I looked up at Montgomery and tipped the box in his direction to show him.

I expected some smartass remark, but instead I

watched him swallow hard, his Adam's apple bobbing.

"What? What does it mean?"

Montgomery looked startled by my question and his eyes met mine. He cleared his throat.

He took out the black collar and motioned for me to turn around so he could put it on. I did and tried not to tremble at the feel of his cool fingers against my warm neck.

"Well, the invitation for tonight is sort of a free-for-all."

I tried to turn so I could look him in the face, but his fingers put pressure on my neck, and he ordered, "Stay still," in a soft voice that immediately had me freezing in place.

He continued to talk while slipping the leather through the clasp and making sure it wasn't too tight around my throat before fastening it.

"Many men tonight will have a female companion, and each of them will be given the choice of what color collar to give their woman. Black means she belongs to her gentleman alone and may not be shared. White means she belongs to everyone at the party and can be used by anyone who wants her."

I couldn't help my gasp at the revelation of that knowledge. My voice got tight as I asked, "And the red?"

I was still looking ahead, Montgomery's fingers

still on the back of my neck even though he'd finished clasping my collar—my *black* collar.

"Red means the female may be shared, but only at her master's choice and with his agreement."

His agreement.

I didn't miss the fact that there was no mention of *the women's* opinion anywhere.

But Montgomery apparently didn't miss *my* silence at his words. He took my shoulders and turned me so that I was facing him.

"We don't force any women to be here," he said. "They choose to be here as much as the men do. As much as you're choosing to be here. We're all adults, and these are the games that adults who can afford to, like to play."

My thoughts roiled for several moments. The fact that he'd brought it up gave me the sense that I wasn't the only one with mixed feelings about all this. But then I smiled and made my face as affable as possible, eyebrows lifted. "I didn't say a thing."

"Oh. Right." He let go of my shoulders and backed away. "Anyway. Let's just go get tonight done. It's good you've already showered. I'll go get ready now." He raked his hands through his hair like he didn't know what else to do with them and then disappeared into the bathroom suite.

Montgomery took a long shower and even longer to get ready so that by the time he appeared in his crisp tux, I had the feeling we were running late.

Mrs. H had been in to do my hair and makeup, not trusting me to do it myself since I'd arrived that first day such a "disaster" in her words. But she was still done before Montgomery appeared from the bathroom, and I heard her *tut tutting* under her breath as she worried the watch face on her wrist.

Montgomery didn't appear to have a care in the world as he strode into the room and reached out an arm for me, though. "No coat tonight," was all he said without ever truly looking in my direction. "They'll expect you to arrive without anything on but the collar."

I clutched the silk robe I'd put on while he was in the bathroom a little tighter. Then I consciously loosened my grip and, after letting out a breath, I slipped out of it and let it pool on the floor at my feet.

Montgomery only slipped and shot me a single, quick glance—and only at my bare ankles no less —before color rose in his cheeks and he looked firmly toward the door, proffering his arm again.

"Come on. Stay by my side. We're fashionably late, but I didn't want to be there for all the beginning small talk and bullshit. The quicker we can get in and out, the better."

Was it just my imagination, or did he seem

nervous tonight? I swallowed hard and a hand strayed to the thick black leather collar at my neck.

"Is everything going to be okay?" I asked in a small voice.

"What?" For the first time in hours, he looked me full in the face, his stern expression softening just the tiniest bit. "Everything will be fine. Just don't leave my side even for a second."

I nodded up and down like a bobble head. He didn't have to tell me twice.

I hurried over to his side and took his arm. The rich, soft fabric of his high-thread-count tux coat was cool and smooth against my fingertips. A shiver went down my spine at the contact, and not just because of the air conditioning on the hot day or even the daunting unknown task that lay ahead.

It was because I was touching him. And if the past had been any indication, tonight we'd be touching a lot more. After a week starved of all contact, I was about to be tossed back into the deep end.

But I was wearing the black collar. He'd chosen it so that *he'd* be the only one touching *me*. It was ridiculous that the thought made my chest warm.

Before I had longer to linger thinking about all the night might hold, Montgomery was striding us toward the door and then out into the hall.

There I was, naked as the day I was born apart from the collar, striding down the smooth, oiled floors of one of the oldest and most well-respected mansions in the whole state.

I would have felt out of place, except that when we got to the grand staircase, there was already a tableau of naked and writhing bodies laid out before us, waiting downstairs in the room below.

My eyes popped wide open, something I immediately regretted considering some of the old, wrinkly, extra fleshy specimens on display.

There was one pot-bellied old man in the corner on a grand wing-backed chair being ridden like the young woman was trying for a barrel-racing championship. Another woman was contorting herself in a feat of gymnastic prowess over two men, one underneath and one on top of her, each of them grunting and humping each of her holes—

"Shut your mouth, dear," Montgomery murmured in my ear and I could hear the smile in his voice. "You'll catch flies."

I immediately clamped my mouth shut.

"How nice that you finally decided to grace us with your presence," bellowed a loud voice from our left.

I looked that way just in time to see a man—the same man I'd seen the first morning I was here with the discarded belle doing the walk of shame. Montgomery's father.

He was shirtless and his— Oh my God, his

half-limp *dick* was just hanging out. Convenient since he'd just stopped having sex with a woman who was still bent over on an ottoman, ass up, to wander over to us at the bottom of the stairs.

Montgomery's jaw locked. "Father."

Montgomery's momentarily light mood was gone. His face was suddenly devoid of emotion, and he kept his eyes fixed on the upper wall, close to the ceiling. I couldn't believe his dad was just walking around like that in front of him. It was obviously something Montgomery didn't want to look at.

But it turned out I hadn't seen anything yet.

"Little birds tell me you've been working harder than ever. Closing deals. Running the office remotely." His father shook his head and grabbed a glass of champagne from a passing waitress with glittering rainbow nipple pasties. The only other thing she was wearing was a thong, and Montgomery's dad made sure to tweak her bare ass before she walked away.

I fucking hated it when customers did that to me. I bet that girl was just trying to make a buck to survive, but these bastards had their hands all over her all night. Considering this party, probably more than that.

Montgomery stayed silent, teeth clenched, eyes on the wall.

His father grinned at him, obviously pleased to

be nettling him. "It seems to me that you're missing the spirit of the Initiation. Or maybe you just chose poorly, if she can't even manage to distract you from your work for a while."

His dad stepped closer to me and reached out a hand toward my chest. An inch before he made contact with my breast, though, Montgomery's hand shot out and caught his father at the wrist. "Look at her collar, Father. You know the rules."

But his father just chuckled. "Ah ah ah. You know everything's a test. The Elders don't look kindly on someone not willing to share their toys. And if you think I'm going to relinquish the keys to my kingdom to someone who can't even play the game... well..."

His father stepped back and pulled his hand away from me. "Maybe you aren't the son I raised you to be."

Finally, Montgomery's gaze shifted. He looked his father straight in the eye.

"Oh, I'm here to play the game. But while some fathers and sons enjoy a particular kind of closeness—" Montgomery's eyes shifted again, and I followed where he looked.

Not far from us a woman was bent over some sort of bench. A young man screwed her from behind while she sucked off an older man from the front. My first instinct was to turn away, but this was the world I was in now, and I forced myself to look closer.

The two men, old and young, shared some distinguishable features. They had the same nose, same hair color, the same build. They had to be father and son. Fucking the same woman at once.

My eyes shot back to Montgomery's father. Was that what he wanted? Had he hoped his son would pick the red or white collar so that I'd be the woman in that position, being taken by both father and son at once?

A shudder went down my spine. I'd known from the beginning that my body would be used in ways I could never have imagined, but *that*? That was a bridge too far. If only because I'd met this man on two occasions, and both times, he'd made me want to crawl out of my skin. I couldn't fathom how Montgomery could be his son.

"That's never been up my alley," Montgomery finished calmly, almost conversationally.

And then he reached down casually and began to finger me. Right in front of his father while they kept talking.

I jumped at the contact but forced myself not to pull away. My face flamed though, and it took everything in me not to wrap my arms around myself and cover up as more and more eyes turned our way.

"You see," Montgomery said, "I thought being a

part of the Order meant that we got to be kings among men. And tonight, as a king, I want all of my pet's attention centered on *me*. Isn't that right, pet?"

He snapped his fingers, the ones that had just been teasing at my sex and pointed at the floor.

And God help me, I dropped to my knees.

This, after all, was the difference between Montgomery and his father. If his father had tried a move like that, I might have spit in his face.

But after our week together and realizing that Montgomery had made an unpopular choice in choosing the black collar... Well, his father was right.

This was a test.

I might not know all that was on the line for Montgomery, but he'd been good to me and I wanted to be good to him in return. I wanted him to succeed. And I certainly wanted him to one-up his bastard of a dad.

So, I didn't just kneel in front of him. I bowed my face flat to the floor with my arms out in front of me in supplication. And readied myself for whatever came next.

13

MONTGOMERY

Wet dreams were made from scenes like this.

Grace, submitting before me, in a position that had my cock throb in need. I had never wanted to fuck someone so badly in my life. I had tried so hard to be a gentleman. I wanted to give the woman the respect she deserved even though we were both thrust into a degrading and sordid nightmare of lust and debauchery.

But I was only so strong.

I couldn't resist the urge to unleash my inner beast forever.

My father stoked the flames, but Grace, in the position she was in, only fueled the fire.

Not thinking, not caring, not feeling anything but an overwhelming desire to pound my cock into her tight little pussy, I unfastened my pants, walked behind her, and knelt down onto the floor like the animal I truly was.

Her pussy lips glistened, her thighs parted even more, and she arched her back as she felt me approach her body. She waited for me, giving herself; she was mine and she fucking knew it.

I took hold of her hair and yanked her head back as I put the tip of my dick to her tight little pussy hole. The dark monster inside of me considered taking her ass, but I would save that treat for another night. For now, her wet pussy would be all I'd need.

With one forceful thrust, I sheathed my cock with her cunt. Balls deep, I groaned loudly, not caring that my father still stood to the side of me. He would grow tired and go find his own pussy to claim, or he wouldn't... I didn't care either way.

Right now, it was about Grace. It was about claiming her as mine. It was about proving to my asshole father that I was indeed a king among men, and this woman taking my cock was my motherfucking queen.

Animalistic. Raw. I fucked her like a lion in heat. Mating with my creature. Mine. I would never share. I would never lend.

My eyes locked on the black collar around her neck, and I knew that would be the only color she'd ever wear. *Black. Black. Black.* My dick would be the only one filling her holes. Only mine. Mine.

Grace's legs trembled, and she began to break position to collapse to the ground. I slapped her ass hard in warning, and when she didn't instantly reposition, I spanked her once again even harder.

"Pose for me, Belle," I demanded as I drove my cock even deeper. I relentlessly fucked her, not giving her a second to recover from one pound after another.

With renewed strength, she pushed her ass out, arched her back, and cried out with release.

"Scream my name," I ordered. "Loudly so everyone can hear who you belong to." I sped up the cadence of my fucking. "Scream it. Now!"

"Montgomery!" she howled. "Montgomery!"

"Who does this pussy belong to?"

"You, sir. You," she replied with an obedience that I hadn't expected but appreciated.

But it wasn't enough. I knew all eyes were on me. I knew all the old dicks were hard and wanted their own turn with my belle. I had to mark my territory. Effectively piss on what was mine.

So, as I got ready to cum, I pulled my dick out and released all over her ass and lower back. My creamy seed dripped down her ass crack and along her lower spine for all to see.

Grace didn't move other than from her heavy

breathing. She allowed my marking to run along her smooth and delicate flesh. Her submission was not lost on me, and I would reward her later.

This belle was mine, and after our public show of dominance and submission... there would be no doubt in anyone's mind.

Did I pass the test tonight?

Hell fucking yes, I did.

I would challenge anyone to fuck like we just did. We ruled this room tonight.

King and Queen.

"That had to be... hard for you," I said, clearly stating the obvious when we returned back to our room.

She had just walked out of the bathroom clean from my cum, and now she wore one of my Harvard shirts and nothing else. I liked seeing her in something of mine. I had this overwhelming need to hold her but kept my distance instead. She most likely needed her space, and I couldn't blame her for it.

She shrugged, but her eyes remained downcast. "We have to do what we have to do."

"Why?" I asked. "I've never asked you why you're doing this Initiation. Is it just because of money?"

For some reason, I didn't believe it was. There was something in Grace's determination that made me believe there was a much larger purpose for her decision to be a belle of the Order.

"You've never been poor," she said as she stared directly in my eyes for the first time since leaving the ballroom. "You have no idea what it's like feeling strangled with the fear of not knowing if you'll have enough money to eat, or to have shelter or to"—she threw her hands up—"just to *live*. There's a constant feeling of hopelessness that you have to fight daily. You live your day to day out of need rather than desire.

"I don't wake up happy." There was vulnerability in her voice as she said it and I wondered if she'd ever admitted it to anyone else out loud. "I never end my day feeling that I had a good day. I'm tired. I'm beaten. I'm just going through the motions of a life I haven't wanted for a while now. And yes, I know that I can work hard and get out of the cycle, but it's not easy. And lately, every time I've tried, I just get knocked back down to where I started."

She let out a loud breath like it was a weight off her chest to confess it all to me.

"You're right," I said. "I don't know what that feels like."

"Do you judge me for it?"

I shook my head. "Not at all. I can't judge you for doing the exact same thing I'm doing. No one knows our stories or our intentions but ourselves."

"But do you think I'm a prostitute?" she asked, and the way her voice cracked while asking told me that she worried I did.

"No." I took a step toward her. "Do you think I'm a monster?"

She shook her head slowly, though I could read in the narrowing of her eyes that she was thinking about my question. "No. Not at all."

"So, then we are both in agreement. We are doing what we have to do for our own reasons. You may be poor, and I may be rich, but we still have reasons that force our hand."

She nodded. "I've always been poor and had to struggle, but that doesn't mean I don't have dreams. Big, *big* dreams. I want the fairytale just like anyone else."

She lifted her arms and motioned around the room. "I want wealth and comfort too. But I wasn't born with it. If I want this kind of life, then I have to make tough decisions to make it happen." Her eyes narrowed as if she were working through everything on the spot.

"Do I want to go through with this Initiation?

Hell no. But at the same time, do I want to go back to waitressing at a crap diner in a crap town? Every day I'd watch my dreams slip further and further away with every dollar tip I may or may not get. No."

She shrugged, her eyes still distant. "Was tonight hard? Yes. But I'll do it again if I have to. I'll do whatever it takes to reach my dream. Because as much as I want to be Cinderella, there is no Prince Charming who is going to come and rescue me. I have to save myself."

So, she wasn't over-romanticizing this and seeing me as her Prince Charming. Good. But every word out of her mouth only had me more intrigued. "What is it you want when this is all over?"

"The same as you," she answered. She stretched her neck like she was getting the kinks out. It was a very natural gesture, but it only emphasized the delicate, feminine slope of her shoulder and throat.

"I want a business to run. I want power. I want money that I earn on my own terms. I want to be the one who decides my fate rather than be at the mercy of some shithead boss. I want to be in control of my destiny and build a legacy of my own. I want to be able to show off my intelligence and be respected."

"Well, you've managed the last part of that

already," I said with a smile. "I see how intelligent you are, and I most certainly respect you. I can see how strong you are. I see your purpose in those green eyes of yours. But I can understand why you want more."

She walked toward the fireplace and stood before it, staring at the empty space where a fire would burn if it weren't such a sticky, hot night.

"I feel dirty though," she admitted in a faint voice. "I don't even think showering will take this away." She sighed deeply. "I know why I'm doing this. I mentally prepare myself for what's to come before every invitation, but it doesn't change the fact that I do feel dirty."

I wanted to steal those thoughts away from her. She should never feel anything but pure and perfect. She needed a distraction before the darkness ate her alive. We both did.

"Why don't we get out of here for a little bit?" I approached her and offered my arm as I had made a habit of doing.

"I don't know about you, but I could use some fresh air." She silently intertwined her elbow with mine and allowed me to escort her out of The Oleander. The fragrance of magnolia, the sound of insects buzzing, and the occasional croaks of frogs set the perfect mood beneath the starry sky.

Normalcy.

Even for a few hours.

As we made our way to the pool, I said, "It's a warm night. I think a swim is exactly what we both need."

I didn't have to say anything more or try to convince her because Grace instantly began stripping down.

Just as she was about to dive in completely naked, she looked over her shoulder at me. "It's not like we haven't been naked in front of each other a few times already. I think we're past all that bashfulness by now."

I chuckled. "Fair enough." I started to undress as I watched her gracefully dive into the pool, cutting through the crystal water with her flawless body.

It was refreshing to jump into the water, but even more so watching Grace swim around me. She didn't worry about getting her hair wet, or messing up her makeup, and I realized right then that I found she didn't care about being manicured, have blown out hair, and being a perfectly painted woman, enticing. It was something that had always been missing in the women I dated before. Arm candy came with a price, and Grace was far from just a sweet piece of confection.

"Do you think anyone will see us?" she asked as she wiped the water from her eyes and smoothed back her slick hair.

"Does it matter?"

"I guess not," she said with a playful smile. "I checked modesty at the door."

"Nothing wrong with being comfortable with your body and sexuality," I said, not caring if anyone saw me swimming naked either.

"Actually... I'm not. Or at least I never was before. I know it might sound nuts considering that I agreed to be a belle, but I'm not exactly promiscuous. I was always the kind of girl who hid my body rather than flaunting it. I don't like the attention."

"That's a shame that you feel that way," I said, swimming closer to her. "You have a beautiful body and should never hide it."

"That's the first genuine compliment you've given me." She laughed as she swayed her arms around in the water in a delicate underwater dance. "Odd really. Everything is so backwards here. We've had sex before even having a full conversation. We've been intimate in ways... well, further than I have ever truly been with anyone, and we haven't even kissed. We aren't following the proper steps of a courtship, Mr. Kingston," she teased.

"Far from proper," I agreed, inching closer. I needed to be near her. The pull was too much. "I apologize for that."

"For what?" Her eyes widened.

"For not giving you what you deserve. I should

have voiced my thoughts which have been filled with silent compliments. And I should have kissed you before we had sex."

"I don't think you did anything wrong." She tilted her head at me. "Considering the circumstances, it wouldn't have been appropriate for you to have kissed me that night or any other time."

Her eyes went distant for a short moment. "Kissing is about feelings. You have to care about someone to kiss them. You should want to with your heart, not just your... Well, you should just *want* to kiss." Her cheeks blushed an adorable pink.

I closed the last remaining distance between us. "But what if I wanted to kiss you but didn't?"

She looked up at me. The droplets of water on her face sparkled with the lights of the pool around us and the dim moonlight above.

"You're gorgeous, Grace. Everything about you captivates my attention. I wish I could give you everything befitting of someone like you. I wish I could treat you with the respect I would if we weren't locked away in this house. I wish that things were different and that I could do it the right way."

In the midst of my world that valued false smiles and never-ending facades, it felt shockingly good to tell the simple truth.

"The right way?"

I boldly ran my fingers through her hair and nodded. "It would have been nice to take you out on a date, bring you flowers, walk you to the door and kiss you goodnight."

"That would have been nice," she softly said, her breath caressing my face.

Our eyes locked, and I could hear nothing but the beat of my heart.

"May I kiss you, Grace?"

With a quick inhale, her lips parted, and her lashes concealed her eyes. "Yes," she whispered.

Moving as slowly as I could, I gently placed my lips on hers. I gripped the back of her head and pulled her into me as I deepened the connection.

Heat coursed through my veins even though we were surrounded in cool water. I wanted more, so much more. But right now, the only thing I would take from this woman was her mouth.

A kiss.

A simple yet powerful kiss.

In private.

Ours and no one else.

This Initiation would only grow in intensity. We would both be pushed to do tasks that neither of us would truly want but we'd still do. But I didn't want to think about the future or The Order of the Silver Ghost.

I only wanted to focus on this kiss.

I wanted to shield Grace from all the eyes, the

lustful thoughts, and the dark desires. She deserved that. She deserved my devotion and respect, and at that very moment, as I dared to dance my tongue with hers, I would only enjoy this private kiss.

14

GRACE

The next week was different than the previous had been. On the surface, maybe it didn't look much different. Montgomery still slept on the floor by the bed and we still didn't talk very much.

But we ate all our meals together and there was just this... easiness between us that hadn't been there before.

He smiled at me in the morning when I woke up. And he always woke up before me. I didn't know how he managed it since neither of us had alarm clocks, but he did.

One day I woke up and found him watching me. He didn't pretend he hadn't been. He just smiled and said, "Good morning, Grace. Sleep well?" all calm, cool, and collected.

But that was Montgomery, wasn't it? Nothing

seemed to ruffle him. Except for maybe his father. But he'd put him in his place so solidly at the last Invitation meeting that a stupid, girlish part of me wondered if there wasn't any obstacle Montgomery couldn't handle.

Dangerous thinking, so I tried to ignore him as best as I could. Thank God for the mansion's library and somebody's affinity for mystery novels. I was working my way through Agatha Christie's entire catalog, along with some Daphne du Maurier.

In spite of my determination to keep my distance from Montgomery, though, I still found myself excitedly explaining the plot to *Jamaica Inn* over a sunny lunch we'd decided to eat on the south terrace.

"It's so much better than *Rebecca*. Why does everyone go on and on about *Rebecca* when *Jamaica Inn* is so much better! There's pirates and ship-wrecks and more going on than just one boring old psycho ghostly ex. Way more dead bodies too, and you know a good thriller always has a respectable body count by the end."

Montgomery laughed. "Can't say I've ever looked at it that way."

But my breath had stopped in my chest from staring at Montgomery.

What had we been talking about again? God, it

was unfair he was so handsome. I bit my bottom lip.

Last night I had a sex dream about him. Totally out of the blue.

He'd just led me down the elegant central staircase and I was wearing the black collar.

But this time there was no one at the bottom of the stairs. It was just us.

He was just as rough and dominant as he'd been that night, though. Taking me with that raw, unbridled need. More passionate than I'd ever known a man *could* be.

I'd woken twisted in the sheets and panting in the middle of the night.

Montgomery was as silent as always on the floor beside the bed. Had I cried out and woken him? Or was he still sleeping and I was being paranoid?

I thought for sure I'd never be able to fall back asleep, but before I knew it, the sun was blazing in the windows and he was there smiling down at me and asking me if I'd slept well. I swear there was a smirk in his eyes as he asked it, though.

"You must like reading," Montgomery said, putting the silver topper over his plate now that he'd finished his meal.

I did the same and leaned back in my chair, feeling stuffed. I'd never eaten so well in my whole life as I had the past couple of weeks.

"I always liked it, but usually I'm too busy. Or other people in the house prefer having the TV on."

My mom had the TV on 24/7 when I was a kid, and the most recent loser I'd been with either had the sports channel on or video games. I didn't know which was worse—probably the video games because that meant he was screaming into his headset at teenagers for half the day and into the wee hours of the morning.

"I like the quiet," I said softly, looking out from the white stone terrace toward the acres of woods that surrounded the property. "What about you? What are you working on? Anything interesting?"

But before he could answer, Mrs. Hawthorne appeared at the pocket doors. She bowed her head to Montgomery and then set both of our plates on a silver tray. Before leaving, though, she set an invitation in front of both Montgomery and me, then left without saying a word. That woman was freakish in her devotion.

Montgomery had been relaxed and easy with me all morning, but now a frown furrowed his brow.

"Go on," I said. "Open it. What are we in for this time?" My heartbeat sped up even as I asked.

At my words, Montgomery came out of his trance and ripped the cream-colored envelope open, yanking out the invitation inside. I did the same and quickly scanned the text.

It looked the same as usual. Our presence was requested in the ballroom at seven o'clock tonight. I didn't see any special instructions.

But Montgomery still looked concerned.

"Is there something I should be worried about?"

Montgomery's eyes were distant, his eyes darting this way and that like he was deep in thought.

"My father will want to reassert his authority over me after my performance at the last Invitation." His eyes came back to me. "Don't underestimate him. He's dangerous."

I picked up my crystal goblet of water and took a sip. "But he can't touch me, right? Because I'm yours?"

Montgomery's eyes went hard. "Don't get your heart set on that. This could get ugly before the end. If I try too hard to protect you, he'll come at us ten times harder."

This time it was me looking away to collect my thoughts. This was all so confusing. He said he couldn't protect me, but he also said "us," like we *were* together in this.

But I'd said it myself. There was no Prince Charming coming to save me. Montgomery was just trying to play it smart and if I were wise, I'd be trying to think as strategically as he was.

"Right," I said, standing up. "I got it. We both just have to do what we have to do to get through this. No hard feelings."

As I started to walk away, though, Montgomery reached out and grasped my wrist. "Grace."

I paused, waiting to hear what he would say. But he didn't follow up with anything and I pulled away, walking over to the pocket doors and waiting silently for him to escort me back down the hallway to our room.

We walked back without another word, the uncomfortable tension that had been dissolved between us the past week returning tenfold.

A box was delivered to our rooms later with two robes. The robe for me was a royal purple sheer see-through number with silk edging, while Montgomery's was a lush, thick silver satin.

We both showered and dressed in silence.

It felt a little like preparing for a firing squad. It was so hard to know how to get ready mentally for these things when you had no idea what was coming.

But it would probably end in sex with Montgomery. In spite of my anxiety about what was coming, a thrill ran through my stomach at the thought. And then immediately soured again when I remembered that his despicable father would likely be looking on.

One thing was for sure, I could damn well use a few belts of that bourbon I always saw the men drinking at these things to calm my nerves. But apparently belles were considered too delicate for drinking or some BS like that? Either way, I hadn't been offered so much as a drop of alcohol since I'd been here.

I snorted as I slipped into the barely-there robe. I'd just bet they'd had to deal with alcoholic belles in the past cause this shit would drive anyone to drink, if only to deal with the nerves.

And then, before I knew it and certainly before I was ready, Montgomery was taking my arm and leading me down that damned staircase.

I sucked in a deep breath and we turned the corner into the ballroom.

But to my surprise, for once, there weren't women and men sprawled out and engaging in all sorts of acts of debauchery.

No, instead, all the Elders and other men in the Order stood around looking solemn in their silver cloaks.

And along the wall in front of the roaring fire in the hearth was a man set up with a—

"Is that—" I started to whisper but Montgomery quieted me with a squeeze on my arm. Instead, he led me closer until my suspicions were confirmed.

It was a small tattoo station. Two chairs were set up, one of which the tattoo artist was already sitting in, along with a little table of supplies including the tattoo gun and a tiny plastic thimbleful of black ink.

I looked up at Montgomery in alarm. "I thought there wouldn't be any permanent damage from this."

His jaw went tight, but he dipped his head so that he could whisper in my ear. "The Order loves to make rules and then test the loopholes. I imagine they'd say that a tattoo isn't technically permanent *damage* since people get them for fun."

I huffed out a semi-panicked breath. Shit. I never wanted a tattoo before. I hated needles. I thought people who got tattoos were crazy to subject themselves to it.

But this is your future. What's an hour or two of pain for your entire future?

Though, could I really trust them to live up to their end of the bargain if they were so casual about finding "loopholes" like this?

Montgomery's father stepped out from amidst the group. "Ah, boy. Here you are. You're up first. Have a seat."

Montgomery's father placed his hands on the

back of the chair opposite the tattooist, a wide grin on his face.

Montgomery didn't skip a beat. He gave my arm another subtle squeeze and then dropped it, striding confidently over to the chair and sitting down.

"Your wrist," the tattooist said. The guy positioned Montgomery's arm and exposed his inner wrist on a little armrest I hadn't noticed before.

No one looked my way or apparently expected anything of me, so I just watched on, biting my bottom lip.

The tattooist prepped Montgomery's inner wrist, shaving the short hairs, placing down the contact paper and then pulling it off again. Left behind on Montgomery's skin was a small, tasteful design of two crossed sabers.

Then came the cringe-worthy part. The buzz of the machine started up and the tattooist slowly began his work. Every few moments, he dipped the tip of his needle in the black ink to absorb more and then continued the line work of the tattoo, swiping away excess ink and blood as he went.

I wasn't sure if it was better to look away or to watch and see what they'd likely be asking me to do next.

In the end, though, it didn't take nearly as long as I expected. The tattoo artist was good at what he did. It was only thirty or forty minutes later when he finished.

He wiped Montgomery's wrist down with anti-septic and then wrapped it in saran wrap and tape.

The Elders stomped their canes in applause as the tradition was completed. Now I wondered if they all had the small sabers tattooed on their wrists. And former belles? Did they have the same? Was I expected to do it now, too?

Montgomery stayed impassive through the entire thing so I couldn't tell if it hurt or not. He stood up and I expected them to call me forward next.

But the tattoo artist began to pack up his equipment.

My eyes shot to Montgomery's, and I could tell he was just as surprised as I was. Was this really just a test for him? I got off scott free for once? I mean, I wasn't complaining or anything, but—

"Now it is time for the Branding of the Belle," Montgomery's father said loudly.

I frowned in confusion.

"Then why is he leaving?" Montgomery asked the question that was on the tip of my tongue. The tattoo artist didn't give us a second glance as he walked out of the ballroom and a few moments later, we heard the slam of the front door behind him.

"You didn't think it would be that easy, did

you?" Montgomery's father taunted him. "We're here to test your mettle, Son. Can you truly do what needs to be done? If so, take up the branding iron and brand your belle as all your forefathers have done before you."

And then the man gestured toward the fire and an item I'd missed before now.

Sticking out from the red-hot flames was what I mistook as a fire poker dug into the embers. But then Montgomery's father pulled it out and brandished it.

The end was white hot and so bright it burned my eyes to look directly at it. But I was able to look long enough to see that the burning end was vaguely shaped the same as Montgomery's new tattoo—in the shape of two crossed sabers.

No.

Fuck no.

I backed away several steps without thinking.

Montgomery moved in front of me, blocking me from the branding iron.

And I suddenly realized that this was about three seconds from all going terribly wrong.

It played out in my mind's eye. Montgomery standing up to his father. Saying that no, that this was barbaric and twisted. Then we'd both be thrown out of the trials and then what?

I'd go back to Nowhere, Georgia, with no money and no future.

And Montgomery. His father would win. I didn't know all the stakes, but I did know that Montgomery would get his father's company if he completed these tests successfully.

But it was a fucking hot iron! They thought they could *brand* me. It wasn't fair! It wasn't what I signed up for.

Ha. So, what else was new?

"She'll get the tattoo," Montgomery was saying to his father while my mind was whirling a million miles an hour. "That's all."

Montgomery's father advanced on him, getting right in his face. "You think you can come in here and start dictating the rules of our traditions? This is exactly what's wrong with your generation and why these trials are more important than *ever*."

He looked back to the rest of the Elders. "Do we want these young bucks coming in and thinking they can do better than us? Better than centuries of established practice and respected tradition? We have to protect ourselves"—he looked back at Montgomery—"even from our own blood, if they aren't willing to participate fully as an equal brother." To the rest of the Elders, he said, "Brotherhood before all!"

"Brotherhood before all," the rest of the gathered men echoed back.

Montgomery's face was red with anger, and I saw him getting ready to argue with his father. It wouldn't get him anywhere. Right now, his dad had the crowd. He'd appealed to their brotherhood, and it would be nearly impossible for Montgomery to frame disagreement with his father as anything other than betrayal to the rest of the group.

"I'll do it," I said, stepping forward before Montgomery could say anything else. And before I could think it all the way through, because that was the only way I would get through this—not thinking. Sometimes your gut told you what was right, and you just had to jump.

Montgomery's head whipped around to look at me, and I saw the conflict in his eyes.

Dear God, I wasn't sure what I was doing, but I didn't back down. I kept my eyes locked with Montgomery's.

I couldn't imagine what it would feel like, couldn't even let myself go there.

But I could look at Montgomery and try to block the rest of the men out to get through this just like I had everything before it.

Montgomery approached me and bent his head. "Say *pearl necklace*," he hissed in a low whisper. "Go. Leave this place and don't look back."

His eyes burned with angry intensity, and I knew it was for me. He was furious on my behalf.

Over Montgomery's shoulder, I saw his father smile in satisfaction. He thought this was it. He thought I would walk away.

But he'd never met Grace Morgan. He didn't know how stubborn I could be.

I met Montgomery's eyes once again. "I trust you."

And then I dropped my robe.

It hurt like nothing I could have imagined.

Montgomery's father tried to wield the branding iron, but Montgomery took it from him, and I was glad. If anyone was going to inflict this wound on me, I knew Montgomery would be the lightest touch.

But it still hurt like the fires of hell when the brand touched the spot on my hip.

I'm not proud, but I screamed. I couldn't help it.

Montgomery pulled the branding iron away almost as soon as he made contact, but the hiss of skin burning was still audible all around the room.

Not even the loud pounding of canes could drown out my screaming.

Montgomery threw the branding iron back into the fire, sending embers and flames flying, and then he picked me up in a cradle-carry and all but ran back up the stairs.

Burn ointment was already laid out on the nightstand beside the bed.

Tears of humiliation burned, thinking of Mrs.

Hawthorne putting it here, knowing before even we did what we'd be facing tonight.

I still had my eyes closed. I couldn't look at Montgomery. He'd just branded me in front of a roomful of men who would have turned on us if he hadn't.

This wasn't a safe place. I thought I could handle it all, that it was worth it, but it hurt so much, and this was all getting out of hand—

I couldn't help the tears that started flowing down my cheeks. It was the first I'd cried since coming here.

"Shit," Montgomery cursed. "I'm so sorry. Grace, you have to believe me. I had no clue that was about to— I'm so sorry."

It wasn't his fault. I knew it wasn't his fault. But I couldn't get the words out to absolve him. I just kept crying.

Montgomery pulled me into his arms and then, when that wasn't close enough, into his lap.

I sobbed into his chest. His strong arms wrapped around me and for the first time all night, I felt safe.

I thrust my face into the soft fabric of his robe, drying the worst of my tears and finally looked up at him. I didn't realize we were so close. Our faces were only inches apart.

And then, where moments ago I'd only been looking for comfort, there was suddenly... *more*.

The intensity of the evening, the rush of adrenaline from the pain, his wanting to save me from it, the circumstances that trapped us both—

I grabbed desperately for his face and kissed him.

He was surprised by it. I could tell in the way it took a moment for him to respond. But then respond he did.

His arms tightened around me and his mouth sealed over mine. It looked like I wasn't the only one with some pent-up feeling and emotion from the evening.

Everything he hadn't been able to say all evening he said in his kiss. He was sorry for my pain. He valued and cherished me.

The pain in my hip was suddenly overshadowed by the euphoria of being in his arms. I buried my hands in his hair, dragging my nails down his scalp. He groaned and shifted beneath me.

"Grace," he moaned low, shifting me in his lap and pulling his lips away to press his forehead against mine. "I need to put the ointment on your burn. I hate the thought of it hurting."

I shook my head and tried to kiss him again, but he just laughed. "Lay back."

I groaned in disappointment, but I did flop back on the bed like he asked.

He went about administering the ointment, applying it with the gentlest fingers. I opened my mouth and then clenched my teeth against the pain, but then moments later the most wonderful thing happened. The burning was replaced by a cool, soothing, numb feeling over the whole area of the brand.

I let out a long breath of relief and flopped my arms over my head. "Can we kiss some more now?"

Montgomery just shook his head at me, wide-eyed. "I've never met anyone like you."

I snorted. "That, I believe."

But Montgomery wasn't laughing. He was looking at me with that dark-eyed intensity I was coming to know well. "In fact, I think you deserve a reward for tonight."

And then he crawled on the bed in between my legs and started massaging my thighs. My *inner* thighs. Upwards toward my—

But he paused before he got anywhere interesting and looked up at me. "Feel free to tell me if I'm out of line."

I just tightly shook my head, barely daring to breathe. "Oh," I managed in a breathy little gasp. "You're fine."

He didn't wait or second-guess himself. He dove face-first into my sex, and I was soon learning that he had talents with his tongue I never even could have guessed.

And a night that started in the worst pain of my life ended in the sweetest ecstasy.

Time...

Grace had to be feeling as if the walls were closing in on her. I sure as hell was. Enough time had passed that I lost count of what day we were on in this self-imposed exile from society. Her branding was healing nicely, thanks to whatever ointment Mrs. H kept giving us to apply. My tattoo was all but healed as well, and for the most part, Grace and I tried to forget that we had a forever mark on our bodies.

Time...

I had never actually spent so much time with one woman unless you counted my mother growing up.

And yet, regardless of how many hours and days Grace and I spent together, the girl was still very much a stranger. A bizarre fact when you considered that we had fucked several times, been far more intimate than I'd ever truly been with anyone else, and we were on this crazy journey together operating as one.

We were teammates, on the same side, and yet, our side was very silent. We didn't have a battle plan because we were going into war blind.

Time...

Long enough to start getting comfortable with each other and the situation, but also each passing day grew more tedious. I was anxious to get back to my life, my business... or what would soon be my business, and to see friends and family again.

I wanted normal not only for me, but for Grace as well. And after the branding, I worried just how much more of this Initiation both Grace and I could endure.

When Mrs. H entered the room with the boxes that would reveal what our night had in store, I could see something different in the way Mrs. H carried her weight and posture.

"You seem tired," I said, grabbing the boxes from her. "When's the last time you had a day off? You need some rest."

She smiled and patted my arm. "Stop your worrying, laddie. I'll rest when one of my boys isn't in the manor going through what you're going through. I owe it to your mother to be here looking after you during all this, and I wouldn't be anywhere else. My place is here at The Oleander, and it always will be."

For the first time since we began the Initiation, Mrs. H actually looked at Grace and gave her a light nod and a weak smile. Grace's wide eyes revealed she also noticed and found the small act of civility surprising.

Mrs. H then said, "I'll be back soon to escort Grace." Without saying another word, she left the room.

"Escort me?" Grace asked as she approached the boxes that I had just placed on the bed. "Why not you? Do we have to be apart? Do I have to do something by myself tonight?"

I shook my head, hating that she sounded anxious. "That's not how this works."

I opened the boxes and instantly knew what the night would have in store from the attire and a single item placed on top of my tuxedo.

I lifted up the chopsticks and used them to point at the kimono that was in the box for Grace. "I actually have attended a number of events growing up around the Order like the one that will happen tonight. I'm pretty sure I know what's going to happen."

She held the kimono to her body and looked up at me, waiting for more explanation.

"It's called *Nyotaimori*. It's a Japanese practice of having a female—you—lying on a table completely naked with sushi, shumai, and sashimi pieces placed all over your body. The men in the room will eat off of you."

Rather than being offended or horrified, Grace laughed, her green eyes sparkling with humor. "Are you kidding me? They want to cover me with raw fish? And you'll all eat this raw fish off of my body?"

I had to smile at her reaction. "It's a favorite here at The Oleander. The Order actually let the sons of the members attend many parties with a sushi girl as the centerpiece. It was the first time I'd ever seen a woman naked."

She laughed again. "This is insane. I actually hope the fuckers get e-coli or something from eating off me. I pray I somehow give them the shits."

My smile turned to a full belly laugh. And as much as I appreciated her lightening the mood, I also wanted to give her the instructions on how to make this situation easier on her.

"They're going to prepare you in a freezer at first. To chill your body. You'll also have to remain as still as you can and stare straight ahead. These men are like sharks. If they smell blood in the water, and even sense you're upset or uncomfortable, they'll try to break you right there on the table. Show zero emotion. None at all. Do you understand?"

When she didn't respond right away, I took hold of her hand and squeezed until she looked me in the eyes.

"It's important that you don't give them what they want. They'll want to see the humiliation and shame on your face. They'd love to see you flinch as they devour the fish inches from your private parts. And they *will* touch you. There is no way around that fact. I can't protect you no matter how much I will want to."

She squeezed my hand back and nodded. "I understand. And as objectifying as this is, I seriously doubt it can be worse than the branding. I got this."

She picked up her kimono and walked toward the bathroom. She paused and looked over her shoulder at me with a warm smile that caused my heart to skip. "*We* got this."

With sake in hand, I sipped as I kept watch over Grace. The sick asshole inside of me loved the sight of her nearly exposed and naked body adorned with colorful sushi and flowers. She was beautiful, and the way her eyes stared at the ceiling as she dutifully performed her role as sushi girl made her even more so. The woman's strength fueled my own. I truly knew I would not be able to survive this without her.

But I also hated watching men walk up to her with their chopsticks, plucking fish off her like she was nothing more than a piece of fine china. Eyes lingered on her tits and her pussy for far too long, and I wanted to gouge their eyes out in retaliation for the act. I hated each and every one of them at that very moment, and there was nothing I could do to stop the party and what they considered to be the highlight.

My Grace for all to feast off of.

The only thing good about the night was that the other recruits were allowed to attend this event, so I at least got to see some friendly faces. They were actually respectful to me by trying to control where their gazes lingered. I appreciated the small display of loyalty.

Walker St. Claire was the first to walk up to where I stood with his own sake in hand. "How's the Initiation going?"

"How do you think?" I answered tersely. "I'm ready for this hell to be over."

"I'm not ready for mine to come up either. But I do look forward to being able to use the political gain I'll get to my advantage."

Walker noticed Sully casually strolling toward us. "Don't let Sully fuck with your mind. He's in a mood for sure. He's sour that he's pulled into this life even though he swore he wouldn't ever be. No escape from our lineage chains."

Sully rarely did formal greetings. Nothing about the man was formal, so when he just cut into Walker and my conversation, I wasn't surprised. "So, can I eat some sushi, or is that like cheating with your girl?" Sully teased with a wicked smile. "I'm hungry but... I'll respect your wishes."

I rolled my eyes and took another sip. "Just stay the fuck away from her."

"Figured as much," Sully said, sipping his sake. "Are you at least getting good sex out of this shit?"

An Elder walked up to Grace and poked at a sashimi right at her pussy. He licked his lips in hunger, and not for fish. My temper grew with every single minute that passed.

"I hope to God you both have huge cocks, because all these old limp dicks will be watching how you fuck. Nothing's private anymore." I knew my tone was prickish, but it took all my might not to punch something.

Sully downed his sake and shook his head. "This is all fucked up. I need something stronger than this shit to drink. I hope it's worth it. I really do."

He didn't say anything else and stormed off on the hunt for anything to help ease his own hatred of The Order of the Silver Ghost.

I should have remained and continued a

conversation with Walker, but I was feeling far from polite at the moment. Without excusing myself, I walked over to the table and leaned down to Grace's ear.

"You're doing great. Stay strong." I wanted to caress her face, kiss her cheek, something to make her feel not so alone in all of this.

I didn't expect for her to answer as I'm sure they all but placed the fear of God into her when they were going over the rules and expectations of what she was supposed to do as they put sushi all over her.

"I've never been one for sushi," my father said as he approached me with a bourbon in hand as well as his chopsticks. "But I may make an exception tonight."

"I heard today that you were meeting with Harrison." I needed to try to distract him for Grace's sake, as well as my own, because if I had to watch him even dare touch her, I very well may punch him in the fucking face.

"I don't know why you are concerning yourself with business while being here," he said as he examined Grace's body with eyes that I wanted to poke out with the chopsticks in his hand. "Especially when you have this delicious piece of meat to eat."

"Harrison is only exporting items off the Black Market now," I continued on with clenched jaw.

"Exactly why I met with him."

"I don't think we need to get mixed up in that bad business. It's a risk that won't pay off."

My father took a piece of sashimi that balanced delicately on Grace's nipple and knocked it off to the table with no intention of actually eating the food but instead just to uncover her body. "Let me worry about what will or will not pay off, Son."

"Even if it risks the business?" I asked, watching how Grace steadied her breathing even though I knew she had to hate the way my father stared at her.

"It takes balls to run an empire."

"It takes intelligence and wise choices," I countered, hating the fact that the man could ignite a rage inside of me that very few could.

My father ran the chopsticks around Grace's nipple, down her stomach and rested the tips right at her mound. There was an expertly placed piece of seaweed-wrapped fish over her clit, and I anticipated him moving it out of the way like he did the one on her nipple, but instead he remained still and looked up at me with a smirk.

"You talk as if the business is yours. It's not. And what you really should be focusing on is your new shiny toy Daddy got you."

He lowered the chopsticks down her slit and scissored them around to spread her folds. Grace remained still even though I wouldn't have blamed her for one second if she were to snap her legs closed or even if she sat up and punched the asshole like he deserved.

But she didn't. She remained perfectly motionless.

"I hate sushi, but I do think I would enjoy the taste of this," my father said as he boldly lowered his mouth to Grace's pussy and licked.

I never knew what feeling homicidal was like until that very moment. He was touching what was mine. He was doing it right in front of me. Taunting me as if this was all a game. And he had a *wife*! My innocent mother... which only made me want to strangle him more.

"Stop," I demanded in a low tone.

The room was loud with conversation, and I didn't want to draw attention our way. It would only fuel my father's need to show off more.

He pulled away and wiped at his mouth as he stood. "Fishy." He put a single chopstick at her entrance and pushed it inside of her. "Not my taste at all."

Grace gasped, her eyes closed, but she quickly composed her position without anyone noticing but my father and me.

He began to push the chopstick in and out of her as he watched me closely. I could tell he wanted to see just how much this bothered me, but I would never give that power over to him.

Instead, I took another drink and swallowed the fury down deep inside of me.

"You care too much about this slut," he said, molesting her hole even more with the utensil, but she didn't move in the slightest. "Which is your first of many mistakes. The belles are nothing but a plaything for us. It's not like they are marrying material or anything. They aren't worthy of anything more than jamming something up inside a hole of theirs. They don't deserve our respect, or even a second thought. They are simply a means to the end."

The chopstick continued to fuck her, and I had to fight the urge to kill. I could only imagine what poor Grace was going through.

"As opposed to the women we marry? Like Mama? You clearly respect her right now."

"Son, you still have so much to learn."

I could never have admitted my true feelings about my father until I began this Initiation. I'd wanted to love him. I'd desperately wanted him to love me. I'd also wanted to make him proud. He was my father, and I had just accepted him for being... well, for being anything but a real father. But I refused to admit how I truly felt about him to anyone, including myself.

Until now...

I hated the fucking man.

He could make me feel so little, weak, and

ashamed with one simple sentence. He treated my mother like shit and had cheated on her their entire marriage no doubt. He violated Grace right in front of me because he knew he could. He had the power, and I didn't. Rage burned inside, and all I could do was watch on.

But I also knew I needed to stop playing his sick game at the moment. A tactical retreat was needed... for now.

His goal was to try to get me to quit or to force Grace to quit, and I wasn't going to allow it to happen. Not on his terms.

So, as hard as it was, I turned my back... on Grace... and walked away. If my father lost his audience, I hoped he would move on to something more entertaining and at least Grace wouldn't have to be fucked with a stick any longer.

And if I didn't walk away, and I didn't go chat with my friends and act like I was enjoying the party, I would break. I would ruin this not only for me, but for Grace. And since the strong woman simply lay on the table, and didn't budge in the slightest, the least I could do was control my temper.

Luckily, the sake was strong and poured freely, because the night ended earlier than normal with all the old fucks stumbling home or to one of the guest rooms to sleep off the stupor.

Mrs. H and some servers had already wheeled

the table with Grace on it out of the room, and I knew she would be upstairs waiting for me. I said my goodbyes to the few friends I had left in the room, and felt the overwhelming urge to punch my fist through a wall.

Storming into the bedroom, I scanned it for Grace, but could hear the shower running in the bathroom. I hated myself. I hated everyone and everything. I wanted to scream. I wanted to beat someone. I wanted to fuck.

And fuck is what I would do.

At least I had some goddamn control over that.

Stripping down, I marched to the bathroom and joined Grace in the shower with no warning, and not asking permission.

The gentleman in me had literally been broken tonight. Now, all that was left was a boiling over inferno of darkness.

Grace jumped in surprise and dropped the soap in her hands. She didn't scream, or demand for me to leave, which was good because it would have been all but impossible to comply. Instead, she took a step away from the stream of water to offer me more room.

I wasn't mad at her. My anger was not directed toward her. But I was pissed as hell. I needed to take it out on someone. And since she was all I had... she would be my prey.

"He touched you," I said as I took hold of the back of her neck, pulling her face to mine.

"He did." Her whisper was barely heard against the sound of the running water.

"You're mine. Mine," I growled as I flipped her wet body around to face the tile wall. I took hold of each of her wrists and placed her hands to help steady her.

She would need it.

My inner demon demanded to take back what was mine.

My father would not be the last man to touch her this night.

"You will be mine in all ways. Always," I proclaimed. She nodded furiously.

I released her wrists and was pleased to see she kept her hands where I had placed them. I took hold of her hips and yanked her lower half toward my hard cock. I wanted her ass out and ready for me. I then took my wet finger and pushed it into her anus without any warning.

She tensed but didn't break her position. "Montgomery..."

"Mine," was all I could say as I inched my finger deeper into her ass, spreading her for what would come next.

Moving my finger side to side, pumping it in and out, I worked her tight little hole in preparation. She moaned and mewled each time I opened her wider, but she never resisted.

My cock throbbed, but I wanted her ready. I wanted to claim this ass of hers. I wanted to make her scream my name. I wanted her to never forget who she belonged to—regardless of what fucker touched her or even looked at her with dark fantasies in their minds.

But her tight little ass wasn't ready. Not for my size... not yet. And since my patience was thin—extremely fucking thin, I shoved my cock into her wet pussy with one forceful thrust.

I kept my finger rooted in her ass as I pounded in and out of her.

I wasn't easy. Far from gentle.

I abused her pussy with every single movement of my hips. I fucked her like I was beating a man—aggressive and hard. I spread that asshole of hers with my hand as I fucked her tiny cunt. My balls slapped against her, and the resonance of shower, wet bodies, and moans of erotic pleasure drove me to the cliff.

"I'm yours," she screamed out as her pussy pulsated around my cock. "I'm yours!"

16

GRACE

I woke up with a start, my arms flying to cover my nakedness. Except I wasn't naked anymore. I was wearing an unnecessarily thick cotton nightgown and now it was covered in sweat.

It had been a nightmare. Just a nightmare.

Except that wasn't true, because I lived through it last night. A long shudder wracked my body.

And all of a sudden, I had to get the hell out of here. The walls were closing in. I didn't know if I could do this anymore.

I glanced over the edge of the bed and saw Montgomery sleeping soundly.

What time was it? The light coming in the window was gray, not pitch black. It must be close to morning. The Manor should be quiet.

I stole out of bed, the opposite side from where Montgomery was sleeping, and pulled on another thick robe and some slippers. Even though I was hot, the extra cover felt like armor in this place where they were determined to constantly strip me naked.

And then, wincing at each creak of the floor-boards, I crept to the door and snuck out.

I'd learned my way around the Manor the past few weeks and found my way to the servant's stair-case Mrs. Hawthorne had led me up that very first evening.

Soundlessly, I ran down the stairs, carefully peeking around the door to the kitchen. Just my luck Mrs. H would be there at whatever ungodly hour of morning this was, sipping tea and just waiting to catch wayward belles.

But all was dark and quiet, and I made a run for it, fleeing for the door off the kitchen. Then finally, blessedly, I dashed out into the freedom of the outdoors.

The second I stepped outside the manor, a huge weight lifted off me.

For a second I glanced toward the driveway and further toward the Avenue of Oaks they were all so proud of, leading away from this twisted place. If I jogged and set a good pace, I could be gone before sunrise.

And then I turned away from it, frowning and confused. Montgomery had taken me down to the lake on the southeast edge of the property on a walk last week, and I fled toward it instead.

When I got there, I was so overheated, I immediately flung off my outer robe. And then I stared at the lake in frustration.

The sky had lightened enough that I could make out the pristine scene of the perfectly placid lake. The birds were just beginning to wake and sing.

It was beautiful. It should be calming and centering me. That was why I'd come here... wasn't it? Or to breathe fresh air untainted by... *them*?

But it wasn't working. Now that I was by myself, everything felt—

It felt—

I was just so—

I couldn't even—

"What are you doing, Grace?" Montgomery's voice was suddenly behind me. He sounded angry. "You don't know what they'll do to you if they find you wandering without me escorting you."

I spun, only to find him standing five feet behind me.

"You followed me?" I asked incredulously.

"When you do foolish things like wander off by yourself, you bet your ass I'll do what it takes to protect you."

"Protect me?" My voice went up an octave. And then I flew at him.

I slammed into him, shoving him hard in the chest. He barely moved at the impact, which only pissed me off more.

I pummeled his chest, all my fury and frustration finally finding a target. He let me. Which was even more fucking infuriating, because I knew my fists were like a small child's to him. I couldn't inflict any real damage.

These bastards were going to break me, and I couldn't even—

I reared my hand back to slap him across the face and he finally grabbed my wrist, halting my arm mid-motion.

And when I looked up into his face, ready to hiss and spit at him, his features were full of only care and concern.

Goddamn him, he wasn't even the target I really wanted to hit and we both knew it. I ripped my arm out of his grasp, hating that I was only able to because he allowed it.

Then I spun and sprinted for the dock jutting out into the lake. I ran with every ounce of strength I had.

Montgomery called out my name from behind me, but I wasn't stopping. I finally knew what I needed.

I jumped off the end of the dock, tucked my knees against my chest, and hit the water with an explosive splash.

I sank down into the dark water and I finally let it all out in the only place I could. I opened my mouth and screamed. The water drowned out the sound of my pain, but I didn't stop.

I screamed and screamed and screamed.

When arms closed around me from behind and tugged me to the surface, I didn't fight.

I was limp. I'd finally found an outlet for my rage, which I hadn't realized was what I'd been looking for all along. Reconnecting with Montgomery in the shower had helped expel some of it, but if I'd kept the rest bottled up anymore, I would've exploded. No matter how futile my cries now were. It wasn't like it would change anything.

Staying still on that table last night while that fuckface violated me with those goddamned chopsticks was the most difficult thing I'd ever done in my entire life and—

I leaned my face back under water and screamed one last time for good measure.

Montgomery rubbed my back and let me scream.

And when I finally sank back against him, he carried me out of the lake, not saying a word. That was good. My mind felt blank finally. I didn't have words and couldn't sort out my emotions.

And being held in Montgomery's arms while he settled us on a stone bench beside the dock felt nice. It felt good to be taken care of for once.

I didn't even complain when he pulled my heavy, sodden cotton nightgown off over my head and helped me into the outer robe I'd thrown off earlier instead.

He'd brought a robe as well and he pulled that on, discreetly slipping out of his wet boxers.

"Grace, I—"

But I shook my head, lifting my legs up on the bench and snuggling into his chest. "Shh, can we just stay like this for a second? It's so quiet," I breathed out, finally feeling all the tension leaving my body in what felt like the first time since forever.

I didn't realize I'd fallen asleep until Montgomery jostled me slightly. I blinked my eyes against the bright sunlight.

"Shit, sorry. I was trying not to wake you. But I didn't want you to get sunburned. If you want to sleep some more, I can get us settled right underneath this oak tree here."

He was being so sweet, my heart squeezed.

"It's okay," I said, suddenly feeling embarrassed about earlier. But then I decided, screw that. "Actually, since we're out here with no eyes or ears on us, could we just talk some before going back?"

I couldn't go back there yet.

Montgomery looked surprised by my request but nodded, setting me on my feet.

I pushed my hair out of my face and cringed to

think how wild it must look after my predawn dip in the lake.

He watched me with wary concern like I might snap again and start pummeling him at any second.

"Grace, should I not have— When we got back to the room, in the shower, was I too rough?"

I barked out a laugh. Did he think that was what this was about? Men were idiots.

"No, that was fine. I mean"—I felt my cheeks heat—"more than fine." But I was still so raw, that wasn't enough. If ever there was a place for honesty, this was it.

I reached out and grabbed his forearm. "It was perfect, actually. It was exactly what I needed in the moment. I needed to get them off me, inside and out. I needed to know I was still a woman and not a... a nameless, faceless *object*. I needed you not to treat me like glass. You were perfect. If you couldn't tell by the way I came like a freight train."

Okay, I couldn't keep meeting his gaze for that last part, but even not looking at him, I could still feel his smile.

When I glanced at him a second later, though, it had dimmed.

"But all this"—his jaw clenched so hard I thought his teeth might crack—"my *father*. It's getting to you."

I huffed out a mirthless laugh. "Yeah, you could say that."

He pulled me tighter into his arms, so that my back was against his chest as we both looked out at the lake. "I fucking hate it."

"But hating it doesn't change anything. And we're still only halfway through." I sighed tiredly.

Montgomery was silent for a long moment, and then he asked tentatively, "I saw you looking at the road when you first snuck out of the Manor. Why didn't you run for it? After last night, why didn't you hightail it down the road and never look back?"

I settled against Montgomery's chest. It was easier this way, somehow. Being cradled in his arms but not having to look at his face.

He was asking the forbidden question. We were never supposed to talk about our hopes and dreams because that meant talking about the future. We were supposed to be nothing to each other after this trial.

Like his father had said last night, I wasn't the marriageable or dating kind. To their blueblood stock, I was just the kind of woman you used and then discarded.

No, Montgomery could never be anything to me other than a partner in the short-term storm. But that didn't mean we couldn't be humans to one another. And humans talked and shared.

So, I opened up to him. I told him about my business classes and how I wanted to get an official, accredited degree. How I wanted to open a restaurant that I hoped in time would double as a sort of community center. "I've planned out the menu of dishes that feel luxurious but are accessible to a wide audience and not just the elite."

Then I looked down at my lap self-consciously. "I know restaurants are notoriously difficult to make a profit on, but I'm not in it to make millions. And I care about the food, but that's because I'm passionate about showing people there are really good comfort foods beyond what you can throw in a deep fryer. I guess I just want to invest in the community and make wherever I end up really feel like home."

Finally, *finally*, I'd have a real place to call home, and I'd create it for others, too.

When Montgomery didn't say anything, I felt a little silly. "Maybe that all sounds really pie-in-the-sky to you."

But I felt Montgomery's body move behind me and when I looked back, I saw him shaking his head. His eyes were full of something I couldn't read. His brow furrowed, and he watched me with this intensity burning from his almost translucent blue-gray eyes. It made my breath catch.

"I've never met anyone who talks the way you do. You're..." He trailed off, shaking his head.

I was still twisted in his arms, my head turned back to look at him. He lifted a hand and pushed some hair out of my face, tucking it behind my ear. I shivered at his touch.

"Nuts?" I offered, giving him a lopsided smile.

He grinned. "I was going to say incredible, but nuts works too."

I smacked him on the arm, but it was light this time, as I turned my head back to the lake and settled into his arms again. "What about you? If you make it through this, then you get your dad's company? Right?"

"Yeah."

"And he's doing illegal shit, but that's not what you want to do."

His arms squeezed me to him a little tighter. "You heard."

"Naked sushi platter, remember? Not much else to do other than listen to passing conversation."

He barked out a laugh. "I can't believe you're joking about that already."

Better to laugh than cry. "Come on, consider this your confessional. How are you going to take that bastard down? It'll help me sleep at night. Especially if there's any way I can help."

"How do you know I have a plan?"

"I've been watching," I confessed. "I'm observant while you work, and I know you're doing more than just returning emails. Tell me... I can help. You can trust me in that."

He took a deep breath and nodded. "Good, because I need you. We're in this together, and I know we can make it out the same way."

"You keep sighing over there," Grace said, looking up from her book that she had been reading most of the day.

"Sorry," I mumbled, directing my attention back to my laptop. "Work shit."

"I'm sure it's hard to try to do the job from this bedroom."

"You have no idea. It doesn't help that my father's a fucking idiot. I don't know if it's that I've been blind before, or if he's just getting careless in his old age, but his risk level is beyond."

"Knowing what I know of your father, it seems like he'd always be shady in how he runs everything in his life," Grace said. "But you'll outsmart him and rise above."

Not being able to focus any longer, and not just because of our conversation, but because I knew

Mrs. H would be coming anytime with our attire for our evening, I closed my laptop.

"The family business is not squeaky clean. Never has been. But things of late seem to cross to a whole new level."

I stood up and began pacing back and forth in front of the window. I felt like a caged tiger.

There was so much I wanted to do. So much I wanted to take over. My plans were detailed, and I needed to feel free to execute them, but I was also far from free. I felt helpless. I could only do so much from my prison, but at the same time, I had to keep plowing through the muck or risk losing any hold I had.

"You must have a lot of your mother in you," Grace said, closing her book and then walking over to me. "You aren't like your father at all."

I don't know if it was the soft and soothing tone of Grace's voice, or the fact that she brought up my mother, but my dark bubble I was drowning in seemed to burst. I couldn't help but smile.

"My mother is an amazing woman. You would really like her, and I know she would like you. She's so kind, giving, and did her best to raise me to be a good man."

"You *are* a good man," Grace said, reaching out to take my hand to cease my pacing.

I took a deep breath in to further calm my tension. "I try to be. Not exactly easy all the time, but I try. I've always wanted to be the best. I guess you could call me an overachiever. Best in school, best in sports, best in business, best in life. But, it seems like no matter what I do, I have this damn Kingston chain yanking me down. The blue blood lineage becomes too much sometimes."

I motioned around the room. "This all becomes too much. I would never treat a woman like I've treated you if I weren't here in The Oleander. Even though I have been all but bred to do so, I would never. My mother would have my balls if I did," I said with a small smirk which quickly disappeared. "I feel like I'm losing a part of me while I'm here."

Grace didn't say anything, but lightly squeezed my hand and nodded.

"And I'm sure you think I sound like some silverspoon-fed asshole who has had everything handed to him, and yet I stand here and bitch about it."

"No," she said softly. "I think you've had to battle demons that I had no idea existed or endured myself. Your story is different than mine, but that doesn't mean you haven't had your hardships as well. I've never thought money means happiness." She chuckled. "But regardless, I still would like some of that money."

Mrs. H knocked on the door before letting herself in right afterwards. She still looked tired, but I wasn't going to say anything about it. She also seemed like she was in a hurry.

"Busy night tonight?" I asked her.

"We're getting invites ready for the next recruit. Sully's up next, and we are vetting the women to be selected." She glanced at Grace and then back at me. "I take this extremely seriously. I want the best belles selected for my boys."

She smiled at Grace and surprised me with her next statement. "The other belles need to live up to this one." She then quickly left the room, not giving Grace nor me a chance to respond.

When the door clicked shut, we both made our way to the bed to see what we would be wearing. When I opened my box expecting to see another tuxedo like I had worn at every other event, I was surprised to see a silver cloak belonging to the members of the Order. I ran my fingertips over the fabric, both excited and terrified.

The days were coming to an end, and I was nearly a full member. Seeing the cloak and being allowed to wear it tonight sent a flurry of emotions —both good and bad—through me. I was born to want this... but my soul was cracking at the same time.

Grace pulled out a blue satin dress with thin spaghetti straps. It was the same color as the ball gown she had worn the night I chose her.

She pulled out a string of pearls as well and

held them up to her neck. "Pretty." She then gave me a smirk. "Are you going to rip these off of me again and ruin them?"

I shrugged. "I have no idea what's in store for tonight. We are now past the point where any recruits have ever attended. So, I haven't been privy to anything beyond."

"We're close," she said, lifting the dress out of the box.

"Very."

"Which means it will most likely get harder and harder."

I nodded as I watched her walk toward the bathroom to change. "I think we can count on that."

When we entered the white ballroom with candelabras circling the room, the flickering candles told me all I needed to know. I was in a silver cloak, as were all the members, so tonight would be more ritualistic than party. Grace wore the only color in the room.

White room. Silver monsters. Blue beauty.

When the canes beat against the floor to announce our entrance, I placed my hand protectively on Grace's lower back to try to offer her some sort of comfort. I watched her take a deep breath and relax her shoulders. Her eyes were focused straight ahead, and this stunning warrior of mine was prepared for battle.

A huge part of me wanted to scoop her up into my arms and carry her out of this house, never to look back again. But this wasn't just about me. I had to remember that Grace had dreams too. This was for her just as much as it was for me.

There was a large structure in the center of the room draped in silver fabric. I couldn't make out what it was, but I didn't have to remain in suspense for long. With the pounding of a cane, a few of the Elders approached the structure and removed the covering.

In the middle of this elegant ballroom that reeked of wealth, class, and elitism, stood a nightmarish sight.

Gallows.

The Elders who had revealed the gallows then approached where we stood and took Grace away from me. They led her up the structure before I could even wrap my head around what was happening.

There wasn't a noose made out of rope hanging from the crossbeam, but instead a noose made out of blue satin—the same exact satin used to make Grace's dress.

Grace's eyes were wide, and her lip trembled as she was turned to face me.

My feet felt as if they were rooted in concrete, and my lungs burned as I struggled for air. I couldn't move. I couldn't scream. I could do nothing but remain frozen in absolute terror.

What the fuck where they going to do to her?

They kept her dress on which surprised me. The first thing I had expected was for them to strip her naked for all to see. One Elder then removed her pearl necklace and handed it to her.

"If you drop the pearls, the evening's trial is over. We will free you from the noose. But if you drop them before the time is up, then the entire Initiation will end as well, and you will leave The Oleander. The choice is up to you," he said.

Grace clutched the pearls with her shaky hand and then looked up at me and gave a very subtle nod. Our connection had reached a point where we understood unspoken words. I could almost hear her telling me to not give up or stop the trial.

She was all in. She would do this... whatever *this* was.

"Montgomery Kingston, this trial is for you as well and will not be easy," the Elder said.

The Elders placed the satin noose around Grace's neck, and I nearly puked. They wouldn't kill her... no way would they... but still...

"Ten minutes and nine seconds. That is the time the trial must last in order for it to be completed. Ten minutes and nine seconds to test both of your resolves. Ten minutes and nine seconds for us to not only try to break the belle but attempt to break you," the Elder continued on. "109 days of Initiation, but the next ten minutes and nine seconds will be a test you both may not be able to endure."

Two Elders approached me, banging their canes as they took every step. I recognized one as being my father. They took hold of my arms and led me to the gallows, right in front of the hatch that I worried would open any minute and drop Grace with the noose around her neck.

Oh God, please don't hang her. Please. This is going too far.

My father then spoke. "The belle will hang for ten minutes and nine seconds. You have the choice to hold her up if you so choose. You can offer her breath, but at a cost. The entire time you hold her up, the Elders will beat you with the canes. *Your* comfort or *hers*. How far will you go to protect the belle? How much will you sacrifice? Do you have the strength to endure?"

The Elders on the platform held on to Grace's arms again, and the hatch opened. They held her, not allowing her to fall.

Her feet dangled, and the only thing preventing her from dropping below were the men.

My father pushed me toward the gallows. "I suggest you go catch her."

Without hesitation, I ran toward the hatch and stood below with open arms as the Elders holding

Grace released her. If I hadn't been there, I feared the satin noose could have snapped her neck, or at the very least, seriously hurt her.

But instead, I was able to break her fall. Although I wasn't tall enough to fully hold her. I was able to wrap my arms around her calves and did my damnedest to keep her lifted high so the least amount of strangulation would occur.

But as I looked up at her, I could see her hands holding around the noose, trying to keep the fabric off her neck.

The pearl necklace remained intertwined in her fingers, and even though it was clear she struggled to breathe, I knew she would have to become unconscious before she would release the strand.

"You drop those pearls the minute you can't breathe!" I shouted up at her. "You hear me, Grace? Drop those fucking pearls if you have to!" I stood up on tiptoes and lifted even higher when I could hear her wheezing for air.

"Ten minutes and nine seconds," I heard my father say.

The Elders surrounded me, and the first strike of the cane hit my lower back.

The surprise of the blow had me nearly releasing my grip of Grace's legs, but I quickly tightened my hold and lifted her even higher.

Another hit on my ass, and then on my thigh, and then on my back once again. Blow after blow, the canes came down on me. There was a cadence to their strikes. An organized assault that had a rhythm as if they were a morbid orchestra creating a symphony of agony.

If I let go of Grace, I knew the beating would stop. But I also knew she wouldn't be able to breathe without my assistance. Even *with* my assistance, I could see she struggled for air.

Sweat dripped off my forehead and burned my eyes as I remained focused on her face. If I saw even the slightest sign of true distress, I would release my hold enough so I could rip those pearls out of her hand myself.

I blocked out the strike after strike of the canes and focused on Grace alone. This was about her. Her only. I would take a beating far longer than ten minutes and nine seconds if I had to. Anything to protect this woman. Anything.

Tears fell down her cheeks and she clung to the satin the best she could to save the pressure against her trachea, but I knew the tears weren't for her own discomfort or fear. She was too selfless to cry over her own agony. She was crying for me.

I watched how she flinched every time a cane came in contact with my body. I saw how her fingers loosened on the necklace each time I was hit.

"Don't watch this! Close your eyes if you have to. I'll be fine," I called up to her, even though my body was ablaze in fiery pain. "Don't you dare release that necklace for my sake. I can take this."

A particularly hard strike connected with my shoulder blade, forcing me to nearly drop Grace. The action was enough that Grace began to claw at her neck, writhe and kick her legs involuntarily as she struggled to breathe. I needed to get her higher now!

Ignoring how another cane connected with my calf to try to throw my balance off even more, I lifted her with all my might. Over and over, the beating continued, but I refused to budge.

I would never let this woman down. Never.

The Elders would have to beat me to death before I would allow them to break me or to break my belle.

And then finally the beating of my body switched to the beating of the floor. All the canes that had been walloping on me, were now in perfect sync as they pounded the white ballroom marble.

The trial was complete.

Ten minutes and nine seconds endured.

My body felt battered, but nothing I couldn't handle.

Two Elders walked up to the noose and cut Grace down. Her body was lowered down to mine, and I held her close as her feet finally made contact with the ground.

I ripped off the noose like it was poison fabric and couldn't get it off her delicate skin fast enough. The noose had left a red mark on her neck, but didn't break the skin, and I was more grateful for that than anything in a long time.

She began kissing me all over my face.

"Are you hurt? How bad are you hurt?" she asked between kisses, not worried about herself, but me instead.

"I'm fine. Just fine." I pulled back just enough that I could inspect her fully and to make sure she was truly okay, but she clearly was doing the same to me.

I then took the pearl necklace that she still gripped in her hand, and draped it around her neck, securing the clasp. She had earned the pearls, and I wanted her to wear them proudly.

Not wanting to be under the watchful eyes of the Elders any longer, and also not giving a fuck what they thought of my actions, I swooped Grace into my arms and charged out of the ballroom.

The trial was over, and I felt no need to inhale the same toxic air with these sick fucks any longer.

"Can you breathe all right?" I asked as she tightened her arms around my neck.

"I'm okay," she said softly. "You lifted me up the entire time, and I could breathe... not well, but I could breathe."

Yes, I'd lifted her up. I would always lift her up.

Something occurred to me this evening as I was beaten repeatedly. This woman I lifted up had been beaten down her entire life.

Far longer than ten minutes and nine seconds.

That would never happen again. Not while I still had my own breath to breathe.

"Thank you," she whispered as she laid her head down on my shoulder.

I glanced down at her in surprise. Why would this woman thank me? I should be begging for forgiveness. I should be on my hands and knees pleading for her not to hate me after everything this poor woman has had to go through. "Why are you thanking me?"

Her eyes locked with mine. "You never let me go."

I slept in a lot that week. Neither Montgomery nor I wanted to admit it, but these trials were taking their toll on us. His body had been beaten nearly black and blue in some areas, and regardless that he kept assuring me that he was fine, I knew his body was tired and needed time to recover.

One morning I found Montgomery in bed with me, just holding me. When I woke up with one of his arms curled around me, he just hushed me and told me to go back to sleep. He had his laptop on the other side of him, and he'd been typing away one-handed as I roused.

"You had a bad dream," was all he said, combing back my hair from my face. "Shh, get some more rest."

Yeah right, I'd thought. Being so close to him

felt too good. There was no way I'd be able to fall back asleep. He went back to his rhythmic typing, obviously thinking I'd drop back off.

But I was awake now. And the feel of his warm, solid thigh against mine, and his strong arm around me... I swallowed hard and squeezed my eyes shut.

Other than the first voyeuristic night as the Elders watched on and the one time in the shower, we'd never... There was that magical morning after waking at the lake but we'd never—

Not in our own bed with no one watching, anyway.

I felt crazy even having the thoughts I was having. Yes, we'd gotten close and the way he was holding me was more tender than any man had ever—

But I was being silly. While Montgomery could be gentle and so sweet in moments like this, he'd never said anything to me besides how beautiful and strong I was. He admired me but was it anything more? Did I want it to be? Hadn't we both agreed this was a short-term partnership and that yeah, we'd be all in while we were here together, but what about after?

Montgomery had never whispered word one to me about the future. And I had the horrible feeling he wasn't making any promises beyond the next few weeks on purpose.

I was the one with the problem. I was the one letting her girlish mind go wild.

"Shh, go back to sleep," Montgomery whispered, again brushing back some hair from my face with the softest touch. His blue-gray eyes were soft as he looked down at me. I locked eyes with him in one breath and with the next, I was slamming his laptop lid shut and wrapping my arms around his neck.

When I pulled him down to the mattress, there was no hesitation. He shoved the laptop down the bed and then shifted so that his heavy body hovered over mine, sliding his thigh in between my opened legs.

"Fuck, you're so goddamned beautiful in the mornings right when you wake up." His head descended and he kissed me full on the lips, still speaking in the low growl that had me liquifying against him.

He moved up to my ear, tugging at my lobe with his teeth. But it was his words that had me surrendering and begging for more of his touch.

"You torment me every night, knowing this lithe, tight little body is right here, so close but so far away."

I shook my head as I dragged his head back to mine. "Not far away right now."

He must have agreed because he shifted his body as he kissed me more deeply than ever, so that I could feel his massive hard-on grinding against the thin fabric of my silk panties. One of my legs was trapped by the covers, but I wrapped the other one around his waist and arched up, giving us both the friction we were desperate for.

Pleasure spiked through me. So hot, so sweet, lightning connected from the tip of his tongue as he teased against the very tip of mine, shooting straight to my sex.

I let out a less than womanly moan of need. I felt desperate for him in a way I'd never experienced before. I scrabbled at the bottom of his white undershirt, desperate for contact with more of his skin. He was apparently on the same page because he jerked it up and yanked it off over his head, descending back on me within moments.

I wrapped my arms around his neck even tighter, clutching his head as he kissed down my neck to my breasts. He pinched and flicked at one nipple while locking onto the other with his sinful lips. Oh God, yes.

"More. Harder." I squirmed restlessly against him, shamelessly rubbing myself against him. And I was already so hot, so needy for his touch, "Oh God, Montgomery."

My nails dug into his scalp as an orgasm lit and then exploded outwards, shocking the hell out of me. I never came that fast or that easily. What the hell?

But Montgomery wasn't stopping or slowing. "Good, that's your first. Let's see how many I can give you at one time."

I whined, already needing more. "Don't you dare tease me. I need your cock. Please, don't make me wait."

He growled and reached down between us. "Vixen, I wanted to take this slow."

I shook my head, still desperately kissing every part of him I could reach. "Slow later. Fuck now."

Except that when he pushed inside me, he grabbed both of my desperate, grasping hands by my wrists and locked them above my head. I immediately whined and squirmed. I needed him. Didn't he get it? I needed it real between us. Tangible. Something more than the farce we were forced to perform in front of others. When he fucked me hard, I felt that. I felt like, for a few minutes in this long, unending universe, I was his whole world.

But Montgomery was always full of surprises and I could no more dictate to him than I could make the earth spin the other way on its axis.

Because where I wanted fast and hard, Montgomery was apparently determined to go slow. I tried to yank my wrists out of his grasp, but he just smiled down at me. And then, his grip as firm as ever, he leaned down just enough to tease the tips of my nipples with his tongue.

It was the most torturous, amazing thing I'd

ever felt. At least until I felt the tip of his cock nudging at my entrance. I tried to angle my hips toward him, nudge closer, but he pulled back every time I did, denying my desires, my way. Without a word, he was silently reminding me he was in control when we were together, whether that was in front of a gallery of onlookers or it was just us.

The realization calmed me down. I trusted Montgomery during the most difficult and trying challenges and now he was silently asking if I could trust him here—in the intimacy of just the two of us.

For a second, I couldn't meet his eyes. Why was this so hard? But he let go of one of my wrists and gently grasped my jaw, tilting my head back so that I met his eyes.

"Where'd you go?" he asked. I left my wrist just where he'd placed it, above my head. Still buzzing with my next orgasm, but on edge because he held me there, a tear slipped down my cheek.

Montgomery looked alarmed and started to pull off me, but I grabbed him, just briefly to let him know I didn't want him to go, then I put my wrists back obediently above my head.

"I want you so badly," I whispered, looking him deep in his blue-flecked gray eyes. Could he hear what I wasn't saying? That I wanted him for longer than just a morning romp. Longer than the next few weeks we had together. That I wanted him more than I'd wanted anything in my life, and it scared the shit out of me. "You're so much more than I— More than I could have ever—"

His eyes softened in the way I adored. "Grace, you're the most precious thing I've ever held in my hands. I'll keep you safe. I swear."

Was I reading into things? Was that the Montgomery version of a declaration of feelings? Oh God, please, I wanted him to feel even half of what I was feeling. Even an inkling of what I was feeling would be enough.

But I was too scared to ask for clarification or press for more.

Instead I gave myself over to him, and for the first time, we didn't just fuck, we made love.

That was two days ago. This morning when I woke, though, Montgomery was nowhere to be seen.

I yawned and stretched, squinting my eyes against the bright light of... I squinted harder, then searched for a clock. What time *was* it? It looked too bright out to still be morning.

Just then the door opened, and Montgomery came in with a tray of food. He smiled when he saw me awake. "Good morning, Sleeping Beauty. Or should I say, good afternoon."

He came over and set the tray at the foot of the bed.

I sat up eagerly, my stomach growling. "Ooo, breakfast in bed. So, this is how the other half lives."

Montgomery rolled his eyes. "Not exactly. I usually eat instant oatmeal for breakfast that I heat up in the microwave on my way out the door. Bachelor, remember?"

I mocked outrage and leaned over to cover his mouth with my hand. "Don't let Mrs. Hawthorne hear that heresy or she'll move in with you so she can cook you three square meals a day."

But Montgomery just tugged me forward by my arm until I landed in his lap. "What about you? Would *you* do something to fix my bachelor ways if you could?"

It felt like his bright, intense eyes were asking about more than just my opinions on his eating habits. Could he be— But I mean, nothing could ever work out between us because he's— and I'm—

I averted my eyes to the tray and frowned when I saw a small white bag stuffed with silver tissue paper beside the food, like it was a present.

"What's that? Is it for me?" I reached for the bag and Montgomery's eyes widened.

"That's for after breakfast," he said, but I was too quick. I snatched the bag and danced away to the other side of the bed.

"Are you trying to keep my present from me?" I giggled, reaching in. My hands closed around an object hidden in the tissue paper and I frowned, not knowing what to make of it. I pulled it out and held it up, laughing. "What *is* it?"

When I looked over at Montgomery, though, his face was red and he had his hand on the back of his neck.

I looked back down at the object of my hands. It looked like a narrow silver egg on a little bejeweled stand, except the egg was slightly pointy on top. I turned it over in my hands. The end of it was covered in jewels that I would have been sure were rhinestones if I were standing in any other place than this mansion. But as it was, I was pretty sure they were inset diamonds and rubies.

"Is it an antique or something? I don't get it."

Montgomery choked a little and then came over to where I was standing. He delicately took the silver egg from me.

"Yes, I guess it is an antique of a sort. It's been sterilized. But um, it's used for... It's um..." His hand went to the back of his neck again.

"What?" I asked, laughing at how embarrassed he was getting.

But his next words had me glad he was holding it, because I might have dropped it in my surprise. "It's a buttplug."

"A *what*?"

Now he was grinning, enjoying that I was the one uncomfortable. "A buttplug. Well, a trainer really. I asked Mrs. H to get it for us because—"

"You asked Mrs. H! For a buttplug!" Oh my God, I was going to die of embarrassment. Staid, solid, Old Country Mrs. Hawthorne had procured me a buttplug. I dropped my face into my hands.

"It's a good thing. You'll be glad for it."

I looked up at Montgomery like he was nuts. "Glad for it?" My voice pitched up an octave higher than normal.

He moved closer, probably sensing that I was near to losing it. "At breakfast we received another invitation."

He pulled out a black collar from behind his back and my tension immediately dissipated. I knew we'd been expecting an invitation any day now since it had almost been a week since the last one—but if it was a black collar night, that meant no one but Montgomery would be touching me. Thank God.

"But they'll be expecting a show. So, I'm going to take your ass tonight."

He stated it so matter-of-factly. I swallowed hard and nodded. I knew there was no escaping this and as much as the idea freaked me out, the fact that it would be Montgomery and no one else... well, it was the only way I was willing to try.

His voice softened. "But I can't stand the

thought of hurting you. Which is why we'll spend the day training you so tonight you can take me." He lifted the egg again.

My eyes immediately widened. When I was just looking at it as an object of curiosity, that had been one thing. But now he was talking about getting that whole thing up my—

I involuntarily took a step back. "Um..."

He lifted an eyebrow and followed me. "Grace," he said in a voice that was half teasing, half warning. "This is happening, even if I have to hold you down."

I paused. Well, actually that sounded sorta hot. I grinned saucily at him. "You promise?"

His eyes flared with heat. "I swear it."

And then he lunged for me, egg in hand. I screeched and tried to leap over the bed, but he caught me by my hips, landing half on top of me.

I giggled and struggled underneath him, but he put his full weight on me, easily pinning me. And God did that feel delicious. Especially when I felt a certain part of him harden. I wiggled my ass extra against him until he was groaning and grinding against me.

This was new. We didn't play like this. But I loved it.

I rolled my ass up against his hardness. "You think you can catch this? You think you can tame this?"

His voice was low and throaty as he reached down and grabbed one of my ass cheeks, giving it a squeeze.

"I think I already own it," he said, tossing up my nightgown and grabbing the flesh of my ass, massaging it with his large hands.

Which sent my libido into fucking overdrive. We hadn't touched each other since the other morning, and it had been driving me crazy.

One of the pillows was on the middle of the bed, since I like to sleep with one between my legs, and it just happened to be positioned right underneath my pelvis at the moment. I ground shamelessly into it, desperate for any sort of friction as Montgomery tugged down my thong and continued massaging my ass.

And his thumbs— Oh God, his thumbs— With each massaging pass, he plunged deeper toward my forbidden place with those damned seeking thumbs of his, until he was prying me open wider than any man had ever dared.

I buried my face in the pillow, embarrassed and thrilled at the intimate things he was doing to me. He was unashamed, so I was, too. It felt filthy and forbidden and... it was turning me on like I never would have imagined.

He paused for a moment, one hand still wedged between my cheeks, and then a moment later I felt a cool, slickness on my backside. Lube. Then his fingers were pushing in even further.

Oh God, oh God, he was—

I couldn't help crying out and thrashing my hips against the pillow when his thumbs finally breached the hole.

"Aw fuck," he swore, sounding lust-drunk off having his fingers up my ass. "Wanna fuck you so bad, beautiful. I want this ass more than I've ever wanted anything on this fucking planet."

The genteel Southern gentleman had left the building. This was my filthy-talking man.

It made me bold. I looked over my shoulder at him, clenching around his fingers in my ass. "Too bad, handsome. You can't have me till tonight."

If I thought he was lust-drunk before, the way his eyes blazed and glazed over with need right then—I wasn't sure I'd be able to stick to my bluff. 'Cause if he wanted to take me right here, right now, I wouldn't be able to say no. My body was already primed for him.

I rocked my hips up and knew I was presenting him with a spectacular view—ass up, wide and ready for him.

For a moment we were frozen, and I thought sure he'd say to hell with it and plunge into me right there—

But the next seconds his warm, strong fingers

retreated from my ass and he grinned when I whimpered at the loss.

"You're right. Good things come to those who wait," he whispered.

And then, before I could really get my bearings or object, cold metal had replaced his fingers. He'd lubed it, I could tell that much because it started sliding in without much problem.

But as it kept going and hit the egg's widest circumference, my eyes widened as big as dinner plates.

Montgomery was there to soothe me, though. "That's it," he murmured, eyes transfixed on my ass. "Almost there. *Allllllmost* there."

Dear God, that tiny egg suddenly felt like an elephant trying to get shoved up my butt!

"No, don't tense up, we're almost there." He started to massage my ass cheeks again. "Loosen up for me."

I breathed out and tried to follow his instructions. Loose. Be loose.

And then, with a little suctioning pop, the egg went in all the way, stopped only by the bejeweled stopper.

"There you go!" Montgomery gave my ass a solid whack that echoed throughout the room. "That's my girl."

I bowed my head into the pillows, only now realizing that sweat was coating my forehead.

Montgomery disappeared into the bathroom, washing his hands probably, and I stayed where I was.

The plug felt... weird. Not bad. But now was I just supposed to walk around all day with this thing up my ass? Oh my God.

Every time he looked at me, Montgomery would know it was there.

I bit my lip. Okay, that was kinda hot.

But when Montgomery came back, he looked as calm, cool, and collected as ever. I sat up, making a face when the egg shifted inside me —*inside me!*—and Montgomery immediately came to my side. "You okay?"

I reached down and ran my fingers along the jewels of the stopper before pulling my underwear back up into place. "Um. Yeah. Totally fine for having a giant egg up my ass. You?"

His eyes darkened. "Probably not going to get any work done today if you keep twitching like that."

I blinked up at him innocently and wiggled my tush against the bed. I still hadn't pulled my night-gown back down, so my long thighs and the small triangle of my thong were visible. "Like this?"

He leaned over and grabbed my face, kissing me long and deep. If I hadn't been intoxicated by lust before, I damn sure was now.

When he pulled away, I reached for him, but he

just laughed and waved a finger in my face. "Ah ah ah," he chastened. "Not till tonight."

And then the bastard had the gall to actually move to the desk in the corner and start to work. Leaving me a needy mess on the bed with nothing but books to distract me all day and a plug up my ass reminding me of what was to come tonight.

19

MONTGOMERY

The box of colored collars sat on the bed again, and I didn't even have to think twice before I reached for the black one, and placed it around Grace's neck, and then attached the leash.

"Don't you think they'll get mad if you keep putting the black one on me?" Grace asked.

"I don't care. It's my choice." I nodded toward the bathroom. "Finish getting ready because we need to get going."

She stripped naked right in front of me and smiled. "What exactly needs to be done to get ready?"

She spun around in a circle as if showing off her nonexistent outfit. She then looked over her shoulder at the plug in her ass. "And how exactly am I supposed to take this out?"

"You aren't," I said with a smirk. "I know most

of the men tonight won't be happy to see a black collar on you again, but at least seeing this little gem planted inside of you will distract them."

She rolled her eyes but didn't argue.

"At least *you* look nice," she said as she straightened my bowtie.

"I'm getting tired of wearing a tux," I stopped short when I realized I had no right to bitch considering she was standing naked with only a collar, a leash, and a butt plug. "But thank you," I added as I leaned down and kissed her softly on the lips. "This will all be over soon."

I didn't even have to tell Grace to get on all fours when we reached the ballroom. This entire situation was clearly becoming second nature to the both of us, and it made me pause and wonder if we would ever be the same once we completed the 109 days. Could we walk out of the manor normal and not be fucked up for the rest of our lives? Maybe this was why my father was such a prick. Maybe The Oleander broke him.

But it would not break me.

And I would not allow it to break Grace.

Mr. St. Claire was the first face I saw when we entered the room. He glanced at Grace, then back at me and offered a small smile before directing his attention to another member of the Order. It was nice to see the black collar didn't bother him, though I knew my father would be a different story.

The party was already beginning.

Cocks were being sucked, pussies being fucked, and asses being spread wide. And yes, we could stand and watch as some were doing, but I also didn't want to place a target on our backs. I wanted to appear as if we were full participants so no one would feel the need to *force* us to get involved.

"I thought I raised you to share your toys, son," my father said from behind me. "But the Elders do have the power to overrule if we so desire."

He squatted down just enough so he could swat Grace on the ass. "Although I do like the piece of jewelry you gave her. Has someone been naughty?"

Grace grimaced, and I knew it was from the disgust of his touch rather than from the sting of the slap. But I admired how easily she regained her control and didn't react further. I wouldn't have been able to be even half as strong as her. He would have been a dead man if the roles had been reversed.

"If you'll excuse me," I said as I tugged the leash to pull Grace closer to my leg. "My pet and I have unfinished business from her earlier attitude and disrespect." I had a good feeling that if I treated her as if she were only mine tonight because I had to punish her, the members would leave both of us alone.

I knew enough about the Order that my dominance would be respected by these men.

My father motioned toward a raised platform—one of many in the room—and said, "By all means. Do your duty."

I should have known he would call my bluff, but by this time, other members had approached as well, so I had no choice but to do exactly as my father wanted. Something in my gut told me it was either me publicly fucking Grace, or one of them, black collar be damned. And I also felt if I didn't give them enough of a show, another might still want a turn as well.

Not getting lost in my head any further, I pulled Grace to the platform and prayed the woman would forgive me for my sins when we were done.

Even though there were a couple platforms occupied with pets and their masters, all available Elders approached ours to watch.

There was no turning back.

Trying to block out the room full of beady little rat eyes staring at me, I unbuckled my belt and pulled it through the loops of my pants.

"You've been a bad, bad, girl," I said for the sake of my audience rather than Grace. I then folded the belt in half and smacked it against my palm.

Grace didn't say anything but I saw her spread her fingers wider on the platform to steady herself.

Not wasting any time, I brought the leather

down upon her bare ass. My force was hard enough to leave a red mark, but not hard enough to leave any bruising... or at least I hoped for that.

She squealed, and I wasn't sure if it was for show or if the act was involuntary. Regardless, I continued on with the spanking. Over and over, I brought the belt down upon her skin, peppering her white flesh until it turned a flaming red. She held position, but I watched how her legs trembled and knew the exact moment when she wouldn't be able to take another whip of my belt.

But I couldn't end the show there. They would want more. And fuck me... *I* wanted more.

I reached into my pocket and pulled out the bottle of lube that I had planned for the night's event. Unzipping my fly, I pulled out my cock that had grown hard by simply watching Grace's bare ass before me.

I knelt down behind her, tugged the butt plug out of her tight little hole and applied more lube. I refused to look up or around the room. My focus was on Grace's ready ass and my throbbing dick.

God help me, I shouldn't want to fuck her ass for all to watch, but my cock disagreed. My body hungered, and I wasn't sure I would be able to stop even if I could without consequences.

I wanted her.

I wanted her now.

"I'm going to fuck this ass of yours," I said as I

positioned the tip of my cock to the puckered flesh of her anus. "And why am I going to fuck this tiny hole of yours?"

When she didn't answer right away, I spanked her punished ass hard as a warning that I expected to *hear* her complete submission. The Order needed to hear it as well.

"Answer me, pet. Why am I going to fuck this ass of yours?"

"Because I'm yours," she mewled. She spread her thighs a little wider in silent permission. "My body is yours to fuck however you choose."

"Good girl," I growled as I eased my way past her tight entrance. She moaned as her flesh stretched around my size, but I didn't stop. She would have to take all of me.

"Mine," I hissed as I buried my cock into her hole inch by inch.

She cried out, and I felt her inner muscles tighten around me. I knew the only way she would be able to enjoy this was if I could get her to relax. I reached around her body and found her clit. Applying pressure and then circling, I paused my intrusion just long enough so she could get used to the size of my girth. When her body seemed to relax slightly, I continued on.

"You're too big," she squealed as she tried to crawl away.

I took hold of her hips with both hands and

planted myself balls deep. She submitted and stilled.

"Whose ass is this?" I began thrusting in and out of her. When she didn't answer, I thrust even deeper.

"Yours!"

When I could see she wasn't going to try to crawl away again, I pressed her shoulders down so her ass was on display and in an even better position to go even deeper inside of her.

"Montgomery, please..."

"Take all of me," I commanded. And though I knew this ass fucking may have been pushing the limits of her pain threshold, I also knew that the buttplug she had worn all day had been preparing her for this moment. "Do you feel me spreading you wide?"

When she didn't answer, I reached forward and took a handful of her hair and tugged her head back.

"Yes, I feel you," she answered obediently, breathlessly.

"Who do you belong to?"

"You."

I pumped in and out of her a few more times, knowing the constricting walls of her ass would be my undoing soon. And although I wanted this feeling to last forever, my need for release took over.

I reached around to find her clit again. She deserved her own pleasure, and I would do whatever I could to make it happen.

"Cum for me, Grace. Cum now."

Her body tensed, and her moans grew louder with every pull and press of my dick. I toyed with her clit more until I could hear, and feel, her impending orgasm.

"Montgomery!"

Her pulsating asshole massaged an erotic explosion from me unlike anything I had ever experienced.

I moaned with one last thrust. Closing my eyes, I selfishly took this moment as mine.

A pretend solitude.

I didn't want to see the faces of my spectators. I didn't want to watch as they repositioned their bodies to hide their own raging hard-ons. I didn't want to see the lust in their eyes. I wanted nothing but blackness. Just the dark.

The dark that I had been accustomed to residing in.

Reaching for Grace, I pulled her to me. I wrapped my arms around her shivering body as she snuggled in close while we both caught our breaths and recovered. My eyes were still closed, but I had Grace with me in my darkness giving me a sense of comfort in our fucked up situation.

Just us.

For now...

I would have to open my eyes soon and face reality. Just like when we left The Oleander, Grace and I would have to face a new reality. One in which we aren't forced to be together any longer.

But for right now, with Grace in my arms, this was my reality.

Eyes closed shut.

That night changed something between Montgomery and me. I always imagined anal sex as a brutal, cruel act. Something guys did to get off because they'd watched it over and over in porn. I never imagined it could amp up the level of intimacy between two people like that...

Or maybe it was the fact that I felt like Montgomery and I shared this secret—like we were the only two people who knew the truth about what was really happening between us, and we were just putting on a performance for everybody else.

We always kept a straight face in front of the staff, even Mrs. Hawthorne, but behind closed doors we joked and giggled and made love.

Sometimes it was casual, but sometimes Montgomery got this intensity in his eyes, even while he'd seemed focused on his work just five minutes before, and he'd come and all but tackle me where I lounged on the bed.

And okaaaaay, it might have something to do with the fact that I stopped bothering to get dressed and at most wore lingerie or a bikini top and short shorts around the room or out to the lake. But to be fair, that was simply because I noticed a directly correlated inverse relationship to the amount of clothes I wore vs. the amount of time Montgomery could go without putting his hands on me.

And like they say, all's fair in love and war.

Except... This wasn't war and it couldn't be love. *Couldn't* be.

I frowned, laying my book to the side of the bed and staring at where Montgomery sat working steadily at his laptop in the corner by the wide open bay window.

Lately I'd taken to working with him. All those business degree classes I took? Turned out they were actually useful. It was fun applying them to real-life situations. I'd helped him come up with a creative solution to figure out a bottleneck in his supply chain the other day. And then I created a flow chart he said was extremely useful to help him and his team visualize and streamline the new production line.

I don't think he said it just to be nice either, because I saw him referring to it throughout the rest of the week. It felt amazing to be seen as more than just "one of the redneck waitresses in the short shorts".

And he was giving me more and more responsibility in the business. He asked my opinions, and our conversations were more candid and even confidential in nature. We discussed his father a lot, and ways we could help counter and even fix situations that were caused by a greedy narcissist. Montgomery was smart... really fucking smart. But he had said several times that I was too. I felt valued, appreciated, and it seemed Montgomery actually benefitted from what I offered.

Then again, Montgomery always made me feel like I was more than my past.

As I watched him now, sunshine poured down on his messy blond bed-head locks. I'd personally arranged that hair myself—by dragging my fingers repeatedly through it and scratching his scalp while he plowed me this morning until I was screeching out my orgasms along with the chorusing morning birds.

A sudden knock on the door startled both of us. I looked to the clock over the door. It was only two in the afternoon. We already enjoyed our lazy lunch in the room and there were never usually visitors at this hour. Not until dinner.

Montgomery's eyes met mine and then he rose swiftly from his chair. "Yes? Come in."

Mrs. Hawthorne's head peeked in the door. "Laddie, your father is here to see you." Her eyes darted past Montgomery to me. "Alone."

I held up my hands to show that I was staying where I was. Montgomery's features went hard but he gave a swift nod. "Where is he waiting for me?"

"In the south dining hall."

"Thanks Mrs. H. Tell him I'll be right there."

She nodded and backed out as quickly as she'd entered, closing the door behind her.

"Is everything okay?" I asked.

Montgomery's eyes were distant, looking out the window. "Huh? Oh, I'm sure everything's fine."

I froze where I sat. For the first time in weeks, Montgomery had just lied to me. Dread trickled through my chest, which had been light just moments ago.

But before I could confront him, he was at the closet door and whipping out a crisp white button up shirt. Because God forbid he talked to his father in just a T-shirt. No doubt the world would end if he did.

I wanted to press him but even in my limited experience with relationships, I knew guys hated clingy, intrusive women. And what if I asked and he just lied to me more?

And the thought hit me—*oh my God, what if Montgomery was playing me?* Was I so desperate, I'd believe anything just because I liked him and wanted to believe what he had to say? Hadn't being with Kyle taught me that guys hung around while they got what they wanted but as soon as something more convenient or easier came along, they moved on?

No. Montgomery wasn't like that...

Was exactly what a naive girl way in over her head would be saying defensively right now. Damn it, I didn't know what to think. I'd always hated stupid girls who ignored signs that things weren't right, and he'd just lied to my *face*.

If I stepped back for just a *second*, even I could see that I was easy and obvious tail right now. But when this trial ended? What then? Montgomery and I had specifically avoided ever talking about the subject.

"I'll be back as soon as I can," Montgomery said, turning to me and pressing a swift kiss to my forehead.

Then, without another word, he was out the door and closing it solidly behind him. He was so smooth. Right from the beginning I'd thought he was too handsome to be kind. And just look at his *father*... what if the apple hadn't fallen as far from the tree as I thought?

I stood, speechless, all alone in the room, for a whole five seconds.

And then I decided that was bullshit.

I was done with unseen forces directing the

course of my life. I so *hoped* Montgomery was a good guy, but what was the harm in gathering a little proof?

I yanked on a soft yoga shirt but didn't bother with shoes. Bare feet would probably serve me better anyway.

I turned the doorknob, eyes half shut, praying I wasn't locked in. They didn't usually lock the door, but then again, they were usually leaving the both of us alone.

But the doorknob turned easily. If Montgomery was supposed to lock it, either he'd forgotten or didn't expect me to try to leave while he wasn't there. Silly man. He should know better than to underestimate me at this point.

The south dining hall. Okay. I bit my lip as I traversed down the hallway. Taking the main central staircase would be a risk but heading down the servant stairway seemed like a surefire way of running into Mrs. Hawthorne.

Aside from Invitation events, the Manor was fairly empty.

I'd take my chances.

On my toes to make the least amount of noise, I sprinted down the hall and hurried down the central staircase, in full view of the entry area and infamous white ballroom downstairs. No one was in sight.

I knew Montgomery and I were lodged in a

room on the north side of the building, so I scampered the opposite direction once I got to the ground floor.

Voices had my feet stilling on the cool wood floor.

I crept closer, looking every direction for anyone who might catch me. The coast was still clear.

"—been impressed with your progress here at the Manor. I wasn't sure you had it in you, but your demonstration at the last Invitation was encouraging."

I covered the last few steps and pressed my ear up against a mahogany door of what I assumed was the south dining hall.

But when I did, the entire door shifted slightly, which is when I realized that it was cracked open. Probably the reason I could hear the voices so clearly in spite of the heavy door. I froze, holding the door as steady as possible.

"I've always been on your side, Dad. I know I don't always do things exactly the way you do, but that doesn't mean we aren't on the same page. All I've ever wanted to do was prove myself to you. I want to work side-by-side with you and prove to you that my vision for the company's future is solid."

I heard the creak of a chair shifting. "I want to build on what you've worked your whole life to create. Isn't that what the Order is all about? Family and legacy? I worked my whole life to be a son you can be proud of."

"That means a lot, Montgomery. It really does. It's true I worried about you. I worried your mother made you too soft."

"You saw for yourself that I'm not soft."

"Then why always with the black collar?" his father pressed. "She's nothing. An object you'll discard once you're done with her. We get bitches like this for a reason. They're no one. If we play a little too hard and break them, no one will notice they're missing. You might not be soft, but I'm not sure you're ruthless enough for the business I've created."

No one will notice they're missing.

There it was in black-and-white. The truth. Not every woman came out of this with a Happily Ever After. What happened to them? The ones they "broke" beyond repair? Were they killed? Hidden away in asylums? I had no doubt the Order had the power to do either and make a person completely disappear.

Oh God, what the hell was I doing? Shoving my head in the sand and pretending to play house with Montgomery? Imagining I was *in love* when this was obviously all just a game to them? One big mind-fuck of a game.

Montgomery's next words only confirmed my fears.

"I have to play both sides," Montgomery said. "I've had to spend more than three months with her. That's the part you don't understand, Dad. Sometimes a deal has to be finessed."

His voice lowered and became more intimate. I had to strain to hear, but I did—I heard every word. "I don't like women when they're screamers and fighters. I prefer to dominate them and have them begging for my cock. I won't apologize for what gets me off."

My heart sank down through the floor.

Yes, Montgomery was smart... really fucking smart.

Montgomery's voice was casual but calculated, like this was a pitch he'd been waiting to make, "It's why I'm the perfect partner for your company. You need a clean, untouchable face if you want to pull off these new deals. Along with a swath of legitimate deals and business to hide whatever else you're doing behind closed doors."

Another creak of a chair.

"Don't you get it?" Montgomery added. "That's me and what I bring to the table. Officially, you'll hand over the business to me, but you'll stay on doing exactly what you are now. It protects the company and insulates us from financial scrutiny.

Why stop at being kings? Together, we'll make more money than God."

With one arm I clutched my stomach and the other I slapped a hand over my mouth. That two-faced golden-tongued liar had been between my thighs this very morning. He'd rocked me to one orgasm after another.

He'd whispered sweet, sweet things to me. We'd made plans.

I'd believed him. Hook, line, and sinker.

Because I was as much a fool as ever when it came to men.

The only thing that could make me any more idiotic would be getting caught right now. So, I spun as quietly as I could and raced back up the stairs to my room.

Ha. Not my room. My prison cell.

And not five minutes later, my handsome warden returned.

Montgomery looked at me speculatively when he came in. I was staring at a page but unable to read it.

He paused when he came in, obviously waiting for me to interrogate him about where he'd been. Act normal. In a den of vipers, I had to learn to be just as duplicitous as every other vile snake here.

"What was that about?" I asked as brightly as possible.

Part of me—a small and very stupid part—hoped that Montgomery would come clean and tell me everything he'd just talked about to his father. He'd explained that it had been a ruse, that he was still just as committed to taking his father down as ever.

"Nothing," Montgomery said breezily, striding back toward his desk and sitting down. "He just wanted to let me know that he was unhappy about me always choosing the black collar. We'll have to do something different the next time a collar invitation comes."

I sat up in alarm. "What does that mean? You'll actually share me?"

Montgomery looked up sharply. "What? No. Never. We'll figure something else out."

I stared at him hard. He seemed so sincere. But then again, he'd sounded just as sincere with his father. He was too good a liar. He'd obviously had a lifetime honing his skills at it. With a father like his, it was no wonder.

But where the hell did that leave me?

I had feelings—and at this point I was able to stop lying to myself, I *did* have feelings, strong ones —for a man who may or may not be a complete mirage.

And two weeks left to survive here, one way or the other.

"Good to see you still standing here," Emmett Washington said as he handed me a glass of scotch.

"Did you think I wouldn't be?" I asked as I stood at the center of attention with my fellow recruits. It had been a couple of weeks since I'd last seen them—although I was beginning to lose all sense of time—and I was pretty sure they all had a million questions for me in order to prepare for their turn.

"It's not easy, right?" Beau Radcliffe asked.

I took a sip of my drink and kept my eyes on the Elders wondering what they had planned for the evening's event. Grace was escorted out of my room by Mrs. H earlier in a beautiful silk dress the color of the sky, and although I had a pretty good idea of what could happen, I still wasn't sure. I had tried to prep Grace the best that I could, but we were operating completely in the blind.

"Where is she? Grace, right?" Rafe Jackson asked as he scanned the room which up to this point was void of any women.

I shrugged. "They took her from our room earlier. I have no idea."

Walker St. Claire approached us with his own drink in hand. "My dad tells me that they have really put you guys through the wringer, and you're actually meeting each challenge head on. He said he doesn't remember it ever being that hard on him, but that he's impressed with how you're handling everything."

"Do I have a choice?" I countered.

"Do any of us have a fucking choice?" Sully cut in, looking his normal pissed off self.

"I'm focusing on the finish line. That's for sure," I said, growing impatient and wanting to know where Grace was. I didn't like being away from her this long without knowing what could be happening to her. "I question my sanity every day and wonder why I do this." I looked at each of my friends before adding, "Why any one of us would do this."

"Tradition," Emmett stated simply.

"Yeah, well, when it's your turn, we'll see how *traditional* you feel."

I couldn't stop worrying about Grace. I should

be with her. We were a team, and although I knew she was one tough cookie, my heart still beat at rapid speed with the unknown.

Where was she? Did she need me? Did she expect me to stop this entire wicked game and be her knight in shining armor? Or did she want me to stand strong just as she was planning on doing? I often wondered if I was expecting too much, or that I would push her past a point of no return... for the both of us.

I just wanted to know where the fuck she was.

Good news was all the Elders and members were in the ballroom, so at least there wasn't some secret Initiation only involving her somewhere, although I wouldn't put it past them to do something like that.

"109 days is a really long time," Walker said. "I really don't know how I'll survive being locked away from society for so long. You guys have to be going crazy."

I nodded as I took another sip, focusing on the burning caused by the scotch in the back of my throat rather than the churning in my gut and the warning bells going off in my head.

Beau looked at Sully. "You're next, my friend. Ready?"

Sully shot daggers from his eyes toward Beau and drank from his nearly empty tumbler rather than answering.

I watched as all the Elders lined themselves in a row in the front of the white room. The lights went out, and an eerie hush cast over us all.

Complete darkness.

A loud staccato of anarchy laced with poison decree.

"Here we go," I heard Sully whisper to my right. "The shit nightmares are made of."

God, he had no idea.

As the canes smashed against the floor, members of the Order lit the candelabras flanking the room revealing a single file of women standing before us. Just like the first night we chose the belles, Grace stood in line searching the room until her eyes locked with mine.

Her green, with my blue, we would fight the black together. Our eyes would not break just as our bodies, minds and souls would also remain intact.

Stay strong, Grace.

Stay strong.

"Gentlemen of The Order of the Silver Ghost," an Elder called out as he took a step forward. "Tonight, is an auction of the belles."

All the Elders struck the floor with their cane to punctuate his statement.

"Only members of the Order may bid on the belles," the Elder said. "One night. One belle.

Highest bid. When the clock strikes twelve, the belle is no longer yours. Let's begin."

No... no... fuck no...

My gut painfully squeezed my inner organs, and bile formed in the back of my throat. I'd had a feeling it would be the auction as the Invitation event tonight. It hadn't occurred yet, and auctions were a favorite pastime of this group.

I had tried to prepare for this. I had even tried to prepare Grace for this possibility as we readied ourselves earlier today.

But to actually hear the words. To stand and watch and not be able to bid on what was mine... mine... fuck no.

"Oh shame. You mean we can't be sick pricks tonight, buy a belle, and fuck her before we all turn into pumpkins at the stroke of twelve?" Sully mumbled. His sarcasm was not lost on me.

My ears rang, and the room spun as I watched the belles before Grace be bid upon and then taken away to a guest room, or to a platform for all to watch as they were fucked as a prize. When it was Grace's turn to be auctioned off, I nearly charged where she stood to swoop her away and to tell all these assholes to go fuck themselves.

But we had a plan. A goal.

We couldn't mess it up now when we were so close. All our hard work would be for nothing. All this time would be lost. I needed to remember why I agreed to do this in the first place.

Focus on the plan. Focus, focus, focus.

It didn't surprise me when my father was the first to bid on Grace. Of course the fucker would. But I was also happy to see that Mr. St. Claire was outbidding my father each time. A bidding war had begun.

"Jesus Christ," Walker hissed. "Why the fuck is my father trying so hard to win Grace? This shit is sick." He took a step closer to me and leaned into my ear. "I'm sorry, man. I don't know why my dad is doing this."

"Better him than my own father," I said, still keeping my eyes locked with Grace's. She didn't move. She didn't tremble. She didn't show an ounce of fear.

Good girl, Grace. Show those fuckers they can't break you.

The Elders were battling it out as if money were no issue. Now it was about who wanted it the most. I refused to watch my father as he fought for his right to fuck Grace however he chose. I feared if I witnessed the evil in his eyes, and the sinister intention painted on his face, that I would have no choice but to strangle him with my bare hands while the entire Order watched.

If my father won the auction...

There would be blood on my hands. I had no

choice but to continue to block out the auction and try to focus on Grace and only Grace. If I didn't tune out all else... I would ruin everything.

"And the winner of the belle is Elder St. Claire," the other Elder finally announced.

I didn't know if I should fall down to my knees in relief that my father had lost, or if I should demand for this all to end immediately.

It was Grace who made the decision for me. With her subtle nod and the stiffening of her spine, she silently spoke. She had this under control, even though I was about to lose it. She would do what it took. The plan. The goal. To the end...

Walker whispered, "I'm sorry. I wish he didn't do this. I'm sorry."

"This is beyond fucked up," Sully said as I watched Walker's dad escort Grace to a corner of the room that was draped in a silver sheet. I could see the faint outline of their shadows behind the fabric but nothing more. It was clear that St. Claire wanted just enough privacy, but still to be present so the entire Order would know he had the belle, and she was his.

Grace was his. I still felt sick, in spite of all my machinations.

"Do you want me to try to stop him? I can demand he leave her alone. Your call. How do you want me to handle it?" Walker asked. "This isn't my Initiation. What's the worst they can do to me?"

"It will just make the situation worse," I answered, watching the silver sheet, hating myself for not being able to look away.

My father approached with a cocktail for himself and another drink for me that he handed off to my shaky grip. He looked at Walker. "Your father sure wanted that piece of ass. It cost him a pretty penny. I was hoping to have her for myself, but whatever." He shrugged as he took a long drink. "A money-hungry whore is a dime a dozen at The Oleander."

When he saw I wasn't drinking from my glass, but obsessing on the silver material cloaking Grace, he nudged me. "Don't let a girl like that get into your head. Just because you were fucking her doesn't mean there was any sort of connection. You know as well as I do that girls like that are good in the bedroom but not marriage material."

He then addressed all the guys surrounding me. "The first lesson you all must gain from your own Initiation is just how little your belle will mean to you in the end. She's in it for the money, just as you are in it for your own gain. It's about greed. Nothing else."

He took another short swing, settling into the self-satisfied role of mentor. "They may make you feel like they are in love with your cock, but they only love your pocketbook and your power. But what makes them different than the woman you will eventually marry is that they'll actually worship you if you can give them a small taste of both."

"Your wife, however," he waved his glass, sloshing some out the sides, "will come from family money and prestige of her own. She won't value your wealth as much but has the ability to make your money shine. Don't *ever* allow a woman to cheapen your value. The belles will do nothing more than flaw the diamond that is your empire. Remember that, boys. That's my tip of the day for you."

Sully huffed. "Whatever."

My father studied the way I looked at the silver sheet. Was that movement I saw? "Shame that St. Claire is a greedy bastard and keeping all of his fun to himself. The least he could do for beating my ass is allow me to watch what I missed out on. Son? Do you want to walk closer so maybe we can at least hear her moans of pleasure?"

"I'm fine where I'm at." It took all my might not to punch my asshole father in the face. He was enjoying this far too much, and knowing that my obvious misery was giving him pleasure made me want to murder him. How he could be so cruel to his own flesh and blood baffled me.

"I saw the way you looked at her. Protected her," my father said. "And I knew you were getting too close. You cared about her whether you wanted to admit it or not."

He pointed to where Grace and St. Claire still remained hidden behind the sheet. "This right here should be a real lesson to you. She could have refused. She could scream for your help right now, and no doubt you would go running to her. She could resist, or even cry out, or use her safe word."

He got right in my face with his liquor-foul breath. "But she didn't. She chose to willingly walk with St. Claire and fuck him for the sake of a pay day. And do you know why?"

When I didn't answer, he continued on. A male groan of satisfaction came from beyond the sheet and I wanted to tear the house down. But in front of my father especially, I would not show one twitch of emotion.

"Because money is all she cares about. She does not care about you. Money is all any woman will ever care about. With wealth comes burden. You can't be a Prince Charming and have your princess too. You'll be used your entire life, and the only way to counter that is to use them first so you don't care. It's the way of the world, boys. Fuck before you're fucked."

Either bored with the conversation, or annoyed he wasn't getting anything from me other than engaging with an emotionless robot who did nothing but stare ahead, my father walked away to find a more entertaining audience.

"Ignore him," Walker said. "He's just trying to piss you off more."

"He has a good point though," Sully cut in. "That woman clearly *is* here for the paycheck." He looked at me, and I could feel his eyes studying me. "Did you really care about her like your father said? If so, I'm sorry, man. This is fucked up."

I shrugged and finally took a long drink. Breaking my stare away from the silver sheet, I refocused my attention back toward my friends. "She has her marching orders, and I have mine. We have to do what we have to do to get through this Initiation."

"You're a shitty liar," Beau said as he patted my back. "But I suppose we'll all have our turn battling the demons we'll be faced with.

Beau was correct.

I was a shitty liar.

I was fucking dying inside.

But Grace and I had a mission. We had loaded the gun, pulled the trigger, and there was no stopping the bullet mid-shot.

The knock on the door had me shooting straight out of bed. Grace stirred but didn't fully wake up. I had been tossing and turning for most of the night trying to get the image of Grace on auction out of my head, so it didn't take much to wake me from my fitful slumber. We had gone to bed barely saying more than a few words to each other.

What was there to say?

We had to do what we had to do. She had to do what she had to do, just as I did.

But would we ever be the same when this was all over? Would the darkness swallow us up completely? As we approached the finish line, the walls were closing in on me and I felt like the suffocation would soon be too much.

"Montgomery?" Mrs. H whispered as she entered the room wearing a robe and slippers. She extended her hand and gave me a cell phone. "I think you better take this call."

She then tiptoed out of the room as I put the phone to my ear.

"This is Montgomery Kingston," I said, anxious to know what was so important to have to call me at this hour. I glanced at the bedside table to see that it was three in the morning.

God, please don't let it be anything involving my mother. Please...

"There's a shipment arriving at the warehouse in an hour that your father is meeting. The Feds know what's on the cargo, and a bust is planned," said a man's voice that sounded familiar, but I couldn't quite recognize.

"Who is this?"

"A friend."

"How do you know about the shipment? Who are you, and how do you know the Feds are coming?" Warning bells were banging in my head.

"Do what you want with the information, but in one hour your father and all the men he's with will be arrested."

A click. Silence.

"Hello? Hello?"

I put down the cell and stared straight ahead as

I tried to process the information from the warning call. How could anyone know about the shipment? I knew it was coming, and I also knew my father had it loaded with so much Black Market shit that it oozed with shady dealings. There was nothing I could do to stop my father while being here at The Oleander, and although I hated what was happening, I was powerless.

But the Feds knew... Father had been sloppy.

There would be a bust...

Running my hand through my hair, I took a deep breath to try to calm my nerves and to formulate a plan of action. Father's ego and his power-hungry greed might fuck up everything.

I immediately tried calling him but there was no answer. I considered calling my mother but there was no point in waking her up and scaring her if there was nothing she could do to stop him. If the shipment was due to arrive in an hour, then he would be out of the house and heading toward the warehouse anyway.

There was only one thing to do. I had to go to that warehouse to stop him myself.

I went back to the bedroom to get dressed. Grace was still sleeping, beautiful in the moonlight that shone through the window.

I crept as quietly as I could over to the dresser and pulled out a pair of jeans and a black cotton shirt.

Part of me wanted to wake her up and explain it all. But what could I say? That I was risking everything we'd sacrificed so much for to go to try to save my jackass of a father?

I'd had a plan. I'd been trying to ingratiate myself to him, pretending to play his games so he'd let me in to the inner workings of the business and I could have a shot at stopping the illegal shit from the inside before it got to this.

But it was obviously too late. He was too far gone and now if I didn't do something...

I tried calling him again, but again, it went straight to voicemail.

Damn it!

Because it only really sunk in then—what I'd have to do and what it would mean.

It was one of the most basic rules of the Trials. Initiates were never to leave the grounds during the 109 days of Initiation. Never. Doing so risked expulsion from the Initiation, no matter how close to the end a person was.

And Grace and I were *one* day away from freedom and all our dreams coming true. The closing ceremonies were tonight. After everything we'd gone through, after all we'd sacrificed, Grace even more than me... What if she hated me?

I froze as I considered what I was risking.

No... I wasn't supposed to leave... but I had to, or my father would go to jail for a very long time.

Losing him in this shameful way would kill my mother. The Kingston name and legacy would be soiled forever in our social and business bubble.

Not to mention, it could ruin the business I worked so hard to build and planned to eventually take over. Everything was on the line.

If I didn't go...

I stared at Grace for a long moment, stopped by her beauty and perfection.

Then I hurried to the desk, scribbled a note promising I'd be back in time, then I grabbed my shoes and was hurrying down the servant's staircase.

The muggy air and the stress of trying to intercept my father before he destroyed our empire had me dripping in sweat. I was happy to see his black Escalade parked in front of our warehouse, and that it wasn't surrounded by flashing lights and gunned law enforcement yet.

Taking the risk that I was on camera, or at least being spotted by the cops' watch out, I casually walked into the warehouse as if it were just an ordinary day. We still had a half hour before the shipment was scheduled, and I needed to convince my father that the intel I received this morning was accurate.

As I walked into the expansive room, my entrance caught the eye of my father and his crew of men. My father's eyes widened as he spun around to face me, and one of his security guards pulled out his gun in reaction to the surprise.

"What are you doing here?" my father asked as he motioned for the guard to put his gun down.

"We need to get out of here now. The Feds set a trap, or they got wind of what's on that shipment."

"What are you talking about?"

I approached closer to the reeling men, prepared to drag my father out of the warehouse if I had to. "I just got a call tipping me off to what's about to go down. We need to get the fuck out of here and not accept the shipment. We need to act like we have no involvement in what's arriving. Say it's not ours. We had no idea it was arriving. Basically, say whatever we need to say, but we sure as hell can't be here when it arrives."

I leaned in closer. "We can deal with the aftermath later, but we need to leave before we all get arrested. No doubt the Feds are on their way, if they aren't already surrounding us." I looked over my shoulder, already paranoid they'd be almost on top of us any second now.

"That's impossible. No way could they know," my father said smugly as he crossed his arms against his chest.

"And what if they do? Are you ready to make

that gamble? You want to go to jail? I sure as fuck don't," I said, feeling as if the timer of a bomb was dangerously close to going off.

"Why would you get an anonymous call and not me?" my father asked.

I struggled not to roll my eyes and start a tirade of curse words directed at the man for his stupidity. "How the hell am I supposed to know that? But we're wasting time standing here."

My father looked toward his men for answers. "How could this have happened?" He looked back at me. "How sure are you that the info you got is good?"

"Sure enough that I'm here saving your ass."

One of my father's men ran toward a window and looked outside. "It's too dark out there to see if we're being watched or surrounded."

Another man spoke up. "Sir, I think the risk is too high. If Montgomery is right, and the police are out there, they can't arrest us if we've done nothing wrong yet. I suggest we leave, regroup, and get our lawyers on this."

My father nodded, but he looked pissed, glaring at me like it was my fault. "Fine, let's get out of here."

He motioned for his men to follow him but paused as he walked directly in front of me. He poked his finger hard into my chest. "You better be right about this. You're about to cost me a lot of fucking money if you're wrong."

"You're welcome," I said through gritted teeth as I turned on my heels and charged out of the warehouse determined to never get this close to dirty dealings ever again.

23

I t was as if the clocks had turned back time. I stood in the ballroom wearing the same tux I had worn the first night of the choosing. Grace stood beside me in her blue ballgown and her string of pearls. We were alone, but I knew it wouldn't be for long.

Tonight, was the final ceremony. We'd reached the end.

I had made it back just in time. I couldn't believe it, but I'd managed to pull it off. I'd seen flashing police lights in my rearview mirror on my way out of the marina.

Once I had left the warehouse, I had no idea if the Feds allowed my father and his men to leave without issue. I hadn't heard from him and had hoped there wasn't any fallout afterwards. But none of that mattered anymore.

Now I was standing here with Grace. And it would soon be over.

"Can you hear my heart beating? I swear it's so loud you can if you listen closely," Grace said in a hushed voice. She'd astounded me when I'd returned earlier. She hadn't been angry, especially after I explained everything. She was supportive, only asking questions about how it had gone and expressing concern about how I was doing.

It was funny. So many in my circle would take one look at her background and think she wasn't good enough for me, but I'd begun to so clearly see it was the other way around. I would have to work my tail off to ever be good enough to deserve her.

"It's going to be okay. Just try to stay calm," I reassured.

"Is it? Is it possible to ever be okay again?"

I didn't respond because I didn't have an answer to that question.

"Montgomery?" she asked in a tiny voice. "If you could do this all over again, knowing what you know now, would you have chosen me?"

"No," I answered automatically. "I would never put you through this, no matter what the payout is in the end." I paused and then asked, "Knowing what you know now, if you got to go back in time, would you have agreed to being a belle?"

"Yes." Her voice was soft at first but then she spoke with more conviction. "Otherwise, I would have never met you. I don't think our worlds would have ever overlapped any other way."

I huffed. "Yeah, welcome to my world. It's a fucked up web of deceit, corruption, and a twisted view of reality. I wouldn't wish this on anyone, and I can't wait until you are safe from all this."

"Even if that isn't what I want?"

"I don't think you truly understand my world," I said sadly. "I don't even think I understand it anymore."

"But you aren't like them."

"How would you even know? You didn't know the man I was before we entered the manor."

I motioned to the room where we stood. "This is my lineage. I was bred for this. I crawled on these floors as a baby. I have the blue blood pumping so thick in my veins that I don't know how to be anything else. And look at me."

When she didn't turn to look at my face, I raised my voice and demanded, "Look at me! I'm my father. He had to go through this Initiation just as his father did. Why would we do this? Why? I'll tell you why. Because we are all sick bastards."

"I don't believe that," she said calmly. "You aren't your father."

"I am. And just like my father, I will someday put my own son through this shit in order to run a business that should rightfully be his. History repeating itself. I'll be one of these Elders someday.

I'll be casting judgment down on some poor soul and try to break him as they have tried to break me. I've tried so hard to resist. You've even helped me not lose every good that I held inside. But I'm tired. I'm fucking exhausted."

As if the Elders could hear us speaking and wanted to arrive on cue, they entered the room in single file. There was a long table in the front of the room, and they each took a seat before us.

Even though their faces were shadowed by the silver hooded cloaks they wore, I was still able to make out the identity of each one. It was an odd relief to see my father's face among them. He'd listened to me after all and made it out in time. The company was safe.

"Montgomery Kingston. Grace Morgan. You both have made it to the final ceremony. 109 days have come and passed, and you met each Trial of the Initiation successfully," one of the Elders announced as he stood and struck his cane hard against the floor as a signal that the ceremony had begun.

The Elder sitting on the far right of the table asked, "Montgomery Kingston, please state to us what your desire is now that you have completed the Initiation."

Finally. It was almost over.

"I choose to take over the family business as the CEO and major stockholder. I also desire to be a full member of The Order of the Silver Ghost. I also would ask the Order to grant Miss Morgan whatever her heart desires. She too has passed the Initiation."

The Elder who first spoke said, "Is there opposition by any of the Elders why Montgomery Kingston should not be granted his right and his claim?"

"I do," my father said as he stood from his seat. "Mr. Kingston has broken one of the rules of the Initiation, hence disqualifying him. He has failed on the final day."

What? If it were possible to be punched in the gut from afar, then it just occurred. I could barely breathe as a shooting pain ran from my heart to my spine.

My father... my own father...

The physical pain caused by betrayal nearly buckled my knees. I'd risked everything to go out to the docks to save him— How could he do this? How?

"He left The Oleander at approximately 3:30 a.m. today. It specifically states in our bylaws that no recruit going through the Initiation may leave the manor for any reason. Due to his breach, he can no longer claim his stake in the business nor join our Order."

"You asshole!" Grace shouted. "He left to save your stupid ass! If it weren't for him, you'd be in jail right now. You owe him your life, you piece of shit!"

I reached for her hand to try to calm her down, but she just brushed it away in her rage.

"What kind of father are you? To betray your own son? After what he did for you?"

My father seemed unfazed by her words. "Regardless of what he did, or why he did it, my son did not follow the rules of the Order. It takes a strong man with a stronger disposition to fully complete the Initiation, and I knew that Montgomery would break eventually." My father spoke with such a disgusted dismissiveness about me.

"And rules are rules. I'm sorry, Son," he went on, not sounding sorry at all, "but you knew what was expected of you when you agreed to the terms of the Initiation. You broke the rules, and therefore the business will remain with me as the CEO and the one calling the shots."

"The business is mine," I snapped. "It's been mine for years. I'm the only one who has busted his ass to try to keep it a legitimate business our forefathers would be proud of. You have done nothing but soil it all in the name of more money."

"Money is what gives us power, Son. It's a shame you're too weak to realize that." He looked around to some of the other Elders, laughing slightly as if he expected them all to agree with him before looking back at me.

"I had hoped you'd be strong enough to show me that you could indeed be a man and pass the Initiation, but my fears have come true. You aren't cut out for it. You've always been softer than me. And I can't protect you any longer. You made your choice when you left, and now it cost you everything."

But someone had tipped me off this morning. My father's position was more precarious than he knew. I refused to back down now. So, it was more to the room that I spoke than to the waste of space that was my father.

"Your money is dirty. You're dirty. I left this morning because I believe in loyalty. I believe in family even though you don't deserve it. You can go to hell. And if this is what the Order is all about, then you are right about one thing. I am not cut out to be a member of it."

Mr. St. Claire pounded his cane against the ground to stop the back and forth argument. "Crime is not what the Order is about. Though our practices may be archaic, barbaric even, sinful in many ways, and ritualistic, the mission has always been to rise above the scours of the land. We are kings and dreammakers, not peasants and thieves. Only the most distinguished and powerful men are part of the Order. Our bloodlines represent respect, prestige, and wealth. Not dirty, back alley deals with men below our pedigree. Call it elite... call it whatever you choose."

My father turned and shot daggers at the man. "St. Claire, with all due respect—"

"Yes, I do deserve respect," St. Claire interrupted. "So kindly sit down and listen to what I say. I speak on behalf of the Elders."

My father scanned the Elders looking for some kind of answer, but the faces of the men remained emotionless. I couldn't read them probably any more than my father could.

St. Claire continued on. "I was the one who called Montgomery and warned him about the impending bust. And yes, the rules clearly state that no one is to leave the manor during the Initiation. But the Elders and I were prepared to make an exception to protect a fellow Elder of the Order.

"We didn't want to see you go down and as these trials are exactly that—a time of testing—we wanted to test just what kind of man Montgomery was before allowing him into our ranks. A selfish man with only his personal interests at stake would have risked nothing, let you be arrested, and assured his inheritance in the Order since your own foolish recklessness would have landed you in prison."

St. Claire glared down Montgomery's father. "What Montgomery showed us instead is that he's level-headed, loyal, wise, with good judgment for the greater good of the group. He put someone else —you—before himself. He is the exact kind of man we need to be part of the Order. If it were not for this recruit, we would have lost an Elder which is not respectable or good for our organization. And rather than you betraying one of your brothers of the Order—not to mention your own flesh and blood—why don't you thank the man before you?"

When my father said nothing but sat with his mouth pursed and arms crossed instead, St. Claire turned his attention back to Montgomery.

"The Order of the Silver Ghost believe that not only did you pass the Initiation, Montgomery Kingston, but you went above and beyond to show your loyalty to the brotherhood. Because of this, your request to take over the company as the CEO and to become a member of the Order is granted."

He then directed his attention toward Grace. "And what is *your* one desire for completing the Initiation, Grace Morgan?"

Grace looked at the Elders, then at me, and then back at the Elders. She didn't say anything for what felt like an eternity, and the silence was confusing me.

She did it. *We* did it.

Why was she not blurting out an atrocious amount of money? Why was she not claiming an amount that would alter her life forever? Her dream was about to come true. What was the hold up? I knew she'd already figured out almost to the dollar how much it would take for her Ivy League education and then to open up a restaurant and support it for two years until it became profitable on its own. Why wasn't she blurting it out?

"I thought I knew what I wanted," she finally said, eyes on the floor and voice quiet before slowly gathering strength as she continued to speak. "When I came into the manor, I had one focus and that was to get enough money to start a business of my own. Money was my end game."

She turned so she could look at me. "But I know if I take the money and walk out that door, I risk never seeing you ever again. You said it yourself... our worlds are different."

She took a deep breath and raised her chin as she stiffened her spine. "I know what I *don't* want, and that's to lose you."

She turned slightly so she could face the Elders. "I've changed my mind on what I want as my one desire. As to my dream."

She refocused her attention on me with tears glistening her eyes.

"I've made my choice. I want to be part of *your* world. I want to continue helping you with the business. All I want is *you*, Montgomery Kingston. Nothing else. I just want you."

Montgomery grabbed me by the shoulders, looked deeply into my eyes, and frowned, shaking his head slightly. "That wasn't the deal."

I held my breath. Shit. I was doing this all wrong. Or worse, what if he didn't want me? What if all this time, he'd just seen us as partners helping each other out—and okay, yeah we'd slept together. But maybe that had only meant something to *me*.

He was just a guy. What guy was gonna turn down free tail? He'd never said a word about commitment beyond the Trials.

And hadn't I heard his horrible father talking while I was hiding behind that awful silver curtain with the elder Mr. St. Claire—

But my spinning brain didn't have time to keep twisting in on itself because Montgomery had hold of my elbow and was pulling me out of the white ballroom, into the foyer, and then out the front door of the mansion.

It was the first time I'd been through the front door.

It was dark and there was a fearsome wind sweeping across the lawn as the moon disappeared behind dark clouds overhead.

"What are you doing?" Montgomery barked. "If you're not careful in there, you'll lose everything. They're literal. They'll give you only what you ask for and not a penny more."

The first drops of cold rain splashed on his sharp, angular jaw, only highlighting his gorgeous face as lightning cracked across the sky.

I didn't know if it was the stress of the past three months or if I was just so emotionally raw now that it was all over—but I didn't have the energy for pretending anymore.

His brow furrowed. "Ever since I met you, all you could talk about was opening that restaurant and making a place in the community for people to gather and—"

It was now or never. I've never been a very brave girl, except for the past few months. I'd taken a leap of faith into the unknown and found more good than bad, even though the bad happened to sometimes be very scary.

But I was still brave enough to jump one more

time. Just one last time. Because Montgomery was worth it.

"I still want that. But I want it *with you*." I reached forward and grabbed his hands in mine. "The truth is I can't imagine any future without you in it."

He didn't respond. His features remained contorted, confused, and his eyes kept darting around past me. Like he was trying to figure out how to let me down slowly. And suddenly the bubble of hope in my chest popped until I felt like I was coated by black goo on the inside.

I yanked my hands back from him, suddenly furious at his confusion and lack of response.

I turned my back to him, pain tearing my chest apart.

"But if that's not what you want, I mean, of course that's fine. I thought..." I swallowed hard, coughing back a painful choke, "I get that this is in real life now and you've got some society wife waiting for you."

"Don't be ridiculous," Montgomery said sharply. "I'm just not sure you're thinking straight. We've been in some hyperintense circumstances and—"

"No," I tried to backpedal. "It's fine. I'll just go in and ask for the money and—"

"See, what did I tell you?" Montgomery's father suddenly appeared behind him on the steps of the mansion. "They're always just in it for the money. She fucked one of your best friend's *fathers* while you were in the room for God's sake. If that's not a whore, I don't know what is. If we never see her again, it won't be too soon.

"Now come on. Take a walk with me, and we'll talk about where we can take the business next. I still think we can salvage some of the dock deal, if we just—"

Montgomery swung his massive shoulders and decked his father, taking him to the cobblestones with a single blow.

His father immediately started screeching expletives, along with indignant cries of, "Do you know who *I am*?"

Montgomery leaned over his father, who was still huddled in the fetal position. "I know exactly who you are. *You're no one.* I will have all your bank accounts emptied by the end of the day. I'm done humoring you or putting up with any of your bullshit now that I don't have to anymore. The business is now mine. Everything is mine."

His words were a balm to my soul. He *had* been pretending with his father that night I'd overheard them. In spite of my momentary doubts, I'd since convinced myself I knew the true Montgomery. I knew his heart. It was still nice to have it confirmed.

His father sat up and sputtered, "You can't do

that. Those accounts are joint trusts between me and your mother."

"About that."

Montgomery gave an arm signal and a car with tinted windows I hadn't noticed arrive at the end of the drive, opened its doors.

A beautiful tall, stately woman with an indefinable elegance walked up the drive. "Hello, Edward," she said coldly.

"Edith," Montgomery's father whined. "Call the lawyer. Call an ambulance. I think my rib's been broken! Help me into the car, darling." He then glared at Montgomery, rage in his eyes. "I'll make you pay for this."

"No, you won't," the woman called Edith said.

"Mama," Montgomery said, "he's not worth it."

Holy crap, she was Montgomery's mother?

But Edith just held up a hand. "You won't be doing anything to our son or me ever again. You've made poor business decisions for far too long and have lost every cent your father left you. All the money we currently have is mine. Not yours. And now that we're getting divorced, I'm holding you to the terms of the prenup."

"Divorced?" Montgomery's father's voice jumped a disbelieving octave. "You can't—"

"Yes, I can," Edith said calmly. "You broke the infidelity clause oh, about a hundred times. More probably. But this time I got you on camera, and is the only one that matters, I suppose. You can thank your son for getting me exactly what I needed while he was here." She tossed an envelope down on top of the still-prone man. "You're getting nothing. Because, *darling*? I want a divorce."

"The Initiation has made Montgomery lose his mind. He's not thinking straight, and whatever he gave you is out of context. I mean look at him... He's not making wise decisions and choosing this white trash girl. She's a whore," his dad shouted, pointing at me. "You're really going to let our son be with a whore? She fucked St. Claire while I watched. If anyone is the cheater here, it's St. Claire. I kept my hands clean. I wouldn't touch her with a ten-foot pole."

My cheeks flamed. He was such a hateful man. I met Edith's eyes and shook my head.

"I didn't have sex with Mr. St. Claire. I swear. Montgomery and I made a plan. We talked it out with Mr. St. Claire ahead of time, in case the auction ever came up because Montgomery didn't want me to have to be with anyone else in the Order. He outbid everyone else—including your husband—to protect me and as a favor to Montgomery. I just went behind the curtain with him, but we didn't do anything other than kick the curtains a few times and make some noises."

I shuddered even at remembering the farce we were forced to enact.

But Montgomery's mother just smiled at me and then at Montgomery. "Jack always did like getting one over on your father." *Jack?* I'd never learned Mr. St. Claire's first name. "He's a good man like that. Unlike my husband."

Montgomery suddenly moved forward, putting an arm around my shoulder. "Mama, it's my honor to introduce Grace Morgan. Grace." Montgomery beamed at me. "This is my mother."

I felt a blush heat my cheeks, but I smiled and extended my hand to clasp hers.

She could not have been more the opposite of Montgomery's father, and I was suddenly glad that he'd had at least one kind influence in his life. I was probably looking at the reason Montgomery wasn't a raging, entitled asshole. I couldn't help it. Emotions were raging so high, I pulled Edith toward me and squeezed her in a tight hug.

When I pulled back, I could see by her eyes that she was moved by the gesture.

Montgomery immediately pulled me back underneath his arm. "Grace and I have been scheming for a while. I couldn't have done this without her strength, intelligence, and dedication." When I looked up into his face, all the confusion from earlier was gone. He was grinning down at me like he was proud and sure of me. Which was now confusing me. What changed?

It made my heart hurt, wanting this so badly.

Wanting *him* so badly. I wanted to be the woman he was proud to show his mother.

But not if it was only temporary.

A heart could only take so much.

Yes, we'd made promises to each other under the tree by the lake.

But they'd only extended to the end of the trial.

We promised never to betray each other. We promised to be honest until the end. He'd told me just how hateful his father was, and he warned me about every Initiation he knew might be coming, and we made plans for how to navigate each one—like the auction. Montgomery knew Mr. St. Claire was tired of his father's irresponsibility and petty cruelties, and arranged ahead of time for him to outbid everyone else.

We'd promised to protect each other and to do whatever it took to support each other so that both of us got through. We would be a team, and we would protect each other *no matter what.*

And then he'd just held me—just held me without pushing for anything more—under the sprawling oak by the sun-dappled lake.

That was when I first began falling in love with Montgomery Kingston. In spite of all the warnings to myself not to. In spite of all my many denials.

I turned away from Montgomery and his mother and swiped at my eyes. I forced a smile I didn't feel before looking back at them.

"Well," I said, trying for cheerful and probably failing miserably. "I should get going. This has certainly been..."

Life-changing. Revelatory. *Heartbreaking.*

"Anyway," I finished lamely. "Maybe I'll see ya."

And then I turned to go.

I didn't make it three feet before Montgomery's arms wrapped around me from behind.

"I couldn't promise you forever back then because it wasn't mine to give. I wasn't free and wasn't sure I'd ever be free of my father. I wasn't going to condemn you to a life by my side always under his thumb. But because of your help, I'm free now. And free to be with you."

And then, before I could quite figure out what was happening, Montgomery had swung me around to face him, and then he'd dropped to one knee. At the same time, he pulled a small box from his pocket.

Was that a— No, it couldn't be—

"What are you doing?" I hissed.

He just grinned at me. "I was waiting for Mama to bring the ring."

My eyes bounced around everywhere. His mother had taken several steps back, but she was watching on with tears glassing her eyes and a smile on her face.

"Will you marry me, Grace Magnolia Morgan?"

"What?" I shrieked, stumbling a few feet backwards.

I caught my balance just in time to see the beautiful gold ring with a single shimmering black pearl in the center, surrounded by diamonds. The light of the front porch danced off of the many facets of the gemstones right as thunder rumbled overhead again.

It was perfect. Exactly what I would've chosen for myself except that I never would have dared to venture into such an expensive part of the jewelry store.

"Is this real?" I whispered.

Montgomery's grin deepened. "We made it. Our happily ever after starts now. Your dreams are my dreams. We'll do all of it. Together. Just like you said. I had to go last night for my father, but even if we'd gotten kicked out of the Trial, I was going to do whatever it took to make it right for you if that happened."

I grinned at him, barely daring to believe all he was saying. I'd understood immediately when he'd explained after getting back. I knew he wouldn't have risked leaving if it had been anything less than an emergency, but to hear that even in the moment of crisis he was thinking about me...

Light rain began to fall all around us.

I'd spent enough of my life chasing dreams not

to grab hold of them when they were right in front of me.

"Yes!" I squealed and then threw myself into Montgomery's arms, kissing him hard on his mouth and then all over his face, again and again and again. Around us, rain began to fall in torrential sheets, but I didn't care. "All I want is you."

A lifetime in Montgomery's arms would still never be enough.

EPILOGUE
SULLY VANDOREN

At least something good came out of this fucked up nightmare of a situation.

Happiness looked good on Montgomery. He deserved it more than most. That man worked hard his entire life for everything he did, and he finally got the outcome befitting of someone like him.

King of his own empire.

With a queen by his side to help rule it.

"I'm surprised to find you here," Beau said as he walked up to where I stood alone and handed me a glass of champagne. "I didn't think engagement parties were your thing. Especially with your own Initiation looming so near."

I took the champagne, seeing that everyone was being served a glass in the room for the upcoming toast.

"It's good to see they both came out of this shit in one piece," I said, noticing that my tone came across harsher than I intended. I didn't want to be the pissed off asshole tonight and ruin a friend's party, so I needed to check my attitude.

"I heard that Grace turned down the money," Beau said as we both looked upon the couple at the front of the room as they stood with champagne glasses in hand. "That's crazy. After all she went through... I guess you could call it love."

That fact alone was why I stood in this room with my mouth shut. I would've found it very hard to celebrate another engagement that I knew was poisoned with Southern money and greed.

Grace seemed different than all the women I knew from around here, and I was happy for Montgomery in finding that rare gem.

A young woman standing next to Grace tapped her flute, the delicate pinging of the crystal getting everyone's attention. Once she felt the eyes of the room were all on her, she cleared her throat to speak.

"Thank you all for coming tonight to celebrate Grace and Montgomery and their engagement. For all y'all who don't know me, my name's Delilah Grace here's my best friend. I've known her a long time, and I couldn't be happier that she finally found a good man. When she first began this... ah, *journey*..."

Delilah paused and gave a smirk to Grace, which she returned. "I sure as fuck—I mean, ahem, I don't think a lot of us thought she'd come out of it hitched and with a new job helping him run his big ass company." She laughed. "I sure as hell didn't expect to get hired on either and finally be free of waiting tables."

She grinned at Montgomery. "But I also didn't expect to be introduced to such a stand-up, honorable, decent guy. These two belong together more than anyone I ever met. So I ask all y'all to raise your glasses to wish them happy ever after as they plan their wedding and dream about their future." Then she leaned in towards the crowd. "And y'all, we gotta get on Grace about popping out some babies sooner rather than later, cause look at these two." She gestured at Grace and Montgomery. "They'd have some *gorgeous* babies, am I right?"

The crowd tittered with laughter and Montgomery's mom actually put her fingers between her lips and let out a whistle. Grace's cheeks were bright red and she was waving at her friend to sit down. Montgomery only sat back and smiled at his fiancée like she hung the moon. I'd never seen the bastard so settled and happy.

Delilah just grinned bigger and raised her glass. "To Montgomery and Grace!"

The room all cheered and clinked glasses, and

even my nasty disposition of late softened. It was hard not to feel the love and pure joy in the room.

Beau clinked his glass with mine and took a sip of his champagne before asking, "So, are you ready for your Initiation?"

"How would one be ready for that?" I asked as I took a big gulp of my own drink to try to dissolve the lump of nerves in my gut.

"If Montgomery survived it, then we all can."

I shrugged. "I suppose." I took a deep breath before adding, "Let the lies begin."

"Well, if your lies are even half as beautiful as Grace, then you won't be too miserable," Beau said with a chuckle.

Lies were lies no matter how you dressed them up. But sure... call them what you want.

Beautiful lies. Ugly lies. It all seemed the same to me. But since I had no choice in the matter but to play along, I would.

Let the *beautiful lies* begin...

Don't stop reading yet.
The Breaking Belles series continues with
BEAUTIFUL LIES (geni.us/BeLi-EN-n).
Are you ready for Sully VanDoren's story?

Want a **bonus scene** of a dark initiation ritual between Grace and Montgomery? For some extra dark, extra sacrilegious sizzle, read the scene that was too dark to make it into the book.
Go to BookHip.com/WPQXMJ to get it NOW!

ALSO BY STASIA BLACK

DARK CONTEMPORARY ROMANCES

BREAKING BELLES SERIES

Elegant Sins [https://geni.us/ElSi-EN-w]

Beautiful Lies [https://geni.us/BeLi-EN-w]

Opulent Obsession [https://geni.us/OpOb-EN-w]

Inherited Malice [https://geni.us/InMa-EN-w]

Delicate Revenge [https://geni.us/DeRe-EN-w]

Lavish Corruption

DARK MAFIA SERIES

Innocence [https://geni.us/Innocence-EN-w]

Awakening [https://geni.us/Awakening-EN-w]

Queen of the Underworld [https://geni.us/
QuOfThUn-EN-w]

The Innocence Trilogy [https://geni.us/InBx-EN-w]

BEAUTY AND THE ROSE SERIES

Beauty's Beast [https://geni.us/BeBe-EN-w]

Beauty and the Thorns [https://geni.us/
BeNThTh-EN-w]

Beauty and the Rose [https://geni.us/BeNThRo-EN-w]

Billionaire's Captive [https://geni.us/BiCa-EN-w]

LOVE SO DARK DUOLOGY

Cut So Deep [https://geni.us/CuSDe-EN-w]

Break So Soft [https://geni.us/BrSSo-EN-w]

Love So Dark [https://geni.us/LoSDa-EN-w]

STUD RANCH SERIES

The Virgin and the Beast [https://geni.us/
ThViNThBe-EN-w]

Hunter [https://geni.us/Hunter-EN-w]

The Virgin Next Door [https://geni.us/
ThViNeDo-EN-w]

Reece [https://geni.us/Reece-EN-w]

Jeremiah

TABOO SERIES

Daddy's Sweet Girl [https://geni.us/DaSwGi-EN-w]

Hurt So Good [https://geni.us/HuSGo-EN-w]

Taboo: a Dark Romance Boxset Collection [https://geni.
us/Taboo_Bx-EN-w]

VASILIEV BRATVA SERIES

Without Remorse [https://geni.us/WiRe-EN-w]

FREEBIE

Indecent: A Taboo Proposal [https://geni.us/SBA-nw-cont-w]

Sci-fi Romances

Draci Alien Series

My Alien's Obsession [https://geni.us/MyAlOb-EN-w]

My Alien's Baby [https://geni.us/MyAlBa-EN-w]

My Alien's Beast [https://geni.us/MyAlBe-EN-w]

Marriage Raffle Series

Theirs To Protect [https://geni.us/Th2Pr-EN-w]

Theirs To Pleasure [https://geni.us/Th2Pl-EN-w]

Theirs To Wed [https://geni.us/Th2We-EN-w]

Theirs To Defy [https://geni.us/Th2De-EN-w]

Theirs To Ransom [https://geni.us/Th2Ra-EN-w]

Marriage Raffle Boxset Part 1 [https://geni.us/MaRaBx-EN-w]

Marriage Raffle Boxset Part 2 [https://geni.us/MaRaBx-2-EN-w]

Freebie

Their Honeymoon [https://BookHip.com/QHCQDM]

ALSO BY ALTA HENSLEY

For all of my books, check out my Amazon Page!

http://amzn.to/2CTmeen

Secret Bride Series:

Captive Bride

Kept Bride

Taken Bride

Top Shelf Series:

Bastards & Whiskey

Villains & Vodka

Scoundrels & Scotch

Devils & Rye

Beasts & Bourbon

Sinners & Gin

Evil Lies Series:

The Truth About Cinder

The Truth About Alice

Breaking Belles Series:

Elegant Sins

Beautiful Lies

Opulent Obsession

Inherited Malice

Delicate Revenge

Lavish Corruption

Dark Fantasy Series:

Snow & the Seven Huntsmen

Red & the Wolves

Queen & the Kingsmen

Mr. D

Mafia Lullaby

Captive Vow

Naughty Girl

Bad Bad Girl

Delicate Scars

His Caged Kitty

Bared

Caged

Forbidden

ABOUT STASIA BLACK

STASIA BLACK grew up in Texas, recently spent a freezing five-year stint in Minnesota, and now is happily planted in sunny California, which she will never, ever leave.

She loves writing, reading, listening to podcasts, and has recently taken up biking after a twenty-year sabbatical (and has the bumps and bruises to prove it). She lives with her own personal cheerleader, aka, her handsome husband, and their teenage son. Wow. Typing that makes her feel old. And writing about herself in the third person makes her feel a little like a nutjob, but ahem! Where were we?

Stasia's drawn to romantic stories that don't take the easy way out. She wants to see beneath people's veneer and poke into their dark places, their twisted motives, and their deepest desires. Basically, she wants to create characters that make readers alternately laugh, cry ugly tears, want to toss their kindles across the room, and then declare they have a new FBB (forever book boyfriend).

Join Stasia's Facebook Group for Readers for access to deleted scenes, to chat with me and other fans and also get access to exclusive giveaways:

Stasia's Facebook Reader Group

(facebook.com/groups/1047415562052038/)

Want to read an EXCLUSIVE, FREE novella, Indecent: a Taboo Proposal, that is available ONLY to my newsletter subscribers, along with news about upcoming releases, sales, exclusive giveaways, and more?

Get **Indecent: a Taboo Proposal**

(geni.us/SBA-nw-cont-w)

When Mia's boyfriend takes her out to her favorite restaurant on their six-year anniversary, she's expecting one kind of proposal. What she didn't expect was her boyfriend's longtime rival, Vaughn McBride, to show up and make a completely different sort of offer: all her boyfriend's debts will be wiped clear. The price?

One night with her.

Website: stasiablack.com

Facebook: facebook.com/StasiaBlackAuthor

Twitter: twitter.com/stasiawritesmut

Instagram: instagram.com/stasiablackauthor

Goodreads: goodreads.com/stasiablack

BookBub: bookbub.com/authors/stasia-black

ABOUT ALTA HENSLEY

ALTA HENSLEY is a USA TODAY bestselling author of hot, dark and dirty romance. She is also an Amazon Top 100 bestselling author. Being a multi-published author in the romance genre, Alta is known for her dark, gritty alpha heroes, sometimes sweet love stories, hot eroticism, and engaging tales of the constant struggle between dominance and submission.

Join Alta's Facebook Group for Readers for access to deleted scenes, to chat with me and other fans and also get access to exclusive giveaways: Alta's Private Facebook Room (facebook.com/groups/886919881448795)

Check out Alta Hensley:
Website: www.altahensley.com
Facebook: facebook.com/AltaHensleyAuthor

Twitter: twitter.com/AltaHensley
Instagram: instagram.com/altahensley
BookBub: bookbub.com/authors/alta-hensley
Sign up for Alta's Newsletter:
readerlinks.com/l/727720/nl